I0547102

The Island of
Ted

...

a novel by
Jason Cunningham

PHANTOM FICTION

PUBLISHING

Nashville

Second Edition: May 2013

ISBN: 978-0-615-42458-3

Editor: Tom Safford

Author Website: http://www.jasonthewriter.com

For Melanie, with love.

No man is an Island, entire of itself; every man is a piece of the Continent, a part of the main; if a clod be washed away by the sea, Europe is the less, as well as if a promontory were, as well as if a manor of thy friends or of thine own were; any man's death diminishes me, because I am involved in Mankind; And therefore never send to know for whom the bell tolls; It tolls for thee.

John Donne, *Meditation XVII*
English clergyman & poet (1572 - 1631)

Part One

"Hollywood is a place where they'll pay you a thousand dollars for a kiss and fifty cents for your soul."

-Marilyn Monroe

CHAPTER

1

If I were a sensible man, I would've been scared to death. Days on end, spent navigating the screens on a Blackberry while pretending to pay attention to whomever had the misfortune of sitting in front of me at lunch or dinner. Two-thirds of my existence involved airports and hotels, and the other third in meetings with people for whom I had little respect. Yet we all bowed to the same god, and his color was green. In the span of only seven years, I had become enslaved to a system that grips its victims without mercy, squeezing the life from their souls, down to the last drop. And worst of all, I had sold myself into slavery.

The stress of work and the frenetic pace of life I'd kept were slowly beginning to kill me. Some nights I was lucky to get four hours of sleep; other nights I didn't sleep at all. Every moment of potential peace was interrupted by the relentless chime of my phone, and I was expected to always answer. I spent hours on end swimming through e-mails and contracts while returning calls from the previous day. To stay in shape, I'd do push ups and air squats while reading screenplays and expense reports. No time for going to the gym, so at least that routine kept me thin. Or maybe it was the constant anxiety that did that.

I'd often find myself at parties, watching celebrities snort lines of cocaine right out in the open as underage groupies traipsed the dance floor wearing dental-floss halter tops. The lifestyle was excessive, and so were the egos. Nothing about my job as a movie producer felt real, except, ironically, being on set. Watching lights being moved into position, sound guys prepping their gear, actors getting into character, the director biting his nails while anxiously awaiting the first shot of the day; being in that atmosphere made me feel like a kid again. And that's what I was missing most these days: childlike wonder.

I often considered if being a producer was worth it, but I didn't have many options. There wasn't much use for a liberal arts degree and the only people I knew were also in the business. My best, and only, friend was my manager and I had no romantic prospects upon which to build any hope. This was life in my world, and always would be: stress, airport lines, dirty hotel sheets, a flooded inbox, and no sleep.

The desire to jump off a bridge and just end it all showed up strong as I sat in a dark and damp screening room at the AMC River East theater in downtown Chicago. My heart fluttered uncontrollably at the thought of failure, even though it seemed inevitable. I felt a tinge of panic when the booming sound dropped to a whisper and I heard shifting weight in the seats—the international sign of boredom.

There were thirteen people in the room but only three of them mattered. I was in the fourth row, my usual spot for such an occasion, while the editor and director sat just below me. The higher you are in the seating arrangement, the more responsibility you carry. I knew the game well after a decade in the business, but it was still a scary time and never got any easier. You see, all of us mid-tier movie producers remember the almost mythical story of Jackie Warner like it had happened yesterday.

Jackie was this producer in the late seventies who was turning out hit after hit. Then he got a bit cocky and started doing his own thing, taking on riskier material. At that point Roger Graham, the head of the studio and the guy I now work for, had a meeting with Jackie behind closed doors. No one knows exactly what was said in that meeting but Jackie came out of the room looking like he'd seen a ghost. That night he jumped off a nine-story balcony and did a face-plant onto Sunset Boulevard, *or so the story goes*.

As my film came to an end, I breathed for the first time in ninety minutes. Dead silence followed. I decided not to draw it out so I twisted in my seat toward the back row where Roger Graham sat, somewhere in the darkness. It would be his decision whether the film would go into three thousand theaters or the bargain bin at Wal-Mart. Adding to my dilemma was the fact that I had no desire to have my brains spilled all over Sunset Boulevard.

There was an uncomfortable silence and then I saw Roger lean forward, puffing on a thick cigar. He dangled a glass of whiskey loosely in his hand. He was an old, hard-nosed curmudgeon who used words like *dame* and referred to movies as *pictures*. I saw Roger as a vestige of Old Hollywood. In an age in which big telecom companies owned most of the movie studios, Roger refused all their offers to insist on getting his own way. And he always did. He was the Godfather of the industry, and no less dangerous.

"How are you feeling, Ted?" he asked in a low, ominous voice that told me to lie.

"Good. I feel pretty good."

There was some discussion at the back of the room but I couldn't hear what was being said.

Roger stood up and gave me a hand signal. He wanted me to follow him. I sprung nervously to my feet and took the long walk up the carpeted floor as every eye in the room fell on me. I looked back over my shoulder and made a joke to lighten the mood.

"Off to the principal's office again."

No one laughed.

I walked into the empty lobby and saw Roger extinguish his cigar on a metal trash can lid. You're not supposed to smoke inside a theater, even one you've rented out, but

Roger did as he pleased and people who questioned him had a strange habit of ending up in the E.R. We were the only two around. Roger took a deep breath and his squinty eyes engaged mine.

"I pulled a lot of strings to get the studio to make this picture. And I put you in charge of it because you're safe; you don't take chances."

"I had to change the ending, Roger. It was just too depressing. If people want to see tragedies and feel hopeless then they can turn on the evening news."

"The game is evolving, Ted. You're not. That was an amateur move. But it's not just the ending."

I was glad that he wasn't yelling, but my neck was still wedged halfway into the guillotine and I smelled blood.

"Here's the thing: we're going in a new direction now. The banks only want to fund our proven money-makers with the economy the way it is. That means romantic comedies and epic action. Everything else is a liability."

It should be mentioned that I had just spent a year of my life producing a heartfelt and profound feature film that was now in danger of never going public due to the cost of advertising, which Roger and I were currently debating—only, it wasn't much of a debate.

"This film can appeal to audiences, Roger. It's about hope. Trust me, people want hope these days. We live in a dark world. We need little reminders like this... reminders that life is still worth living. Hell, I need this."

"Ted, this isn't open mic at the Poetry Corner. Save your spiel for the hippies. I let you run with this picture because the story was good and you know how to get us in on budget. But that's not enough anymore. The landscape has changed."

Roger ran his meaty hand across his face and lowered his eyes.

"Are we even getting a release?"

"I don't know, Ted. But it doesn't look good."

My anger flared. I debated in my head whether or not I wanted to push the issue with a guy you'd rather not piss off, but there was a momentary loss of communication between my brain and tongue.

It came out in a hushed yell. "I put everything into this film, Roger. How could we not get a release? It's the first movie I'm not ashamed to put my name on."

"Listen," he said, softening a bit. "It's a fine picture. There should be some comfort in knowing that. It's just not commercial enough."

"Roger, it's just that…" I stumbled, searching for the words. "I thought we could change the way things are done in Hollywood, you know?"

Roger stared at me for so long without talking, or blinking, that I thought about taking a step backward.

"Tell me," he said. "How long have you worked underneath my large and generous wing?"

"Since grad school, sir. Seven, eight years?"

"And you've been wanting to change the world since I met you." He took a dramatic pause, then continued, "Maybe this business isn't right for that."

Was he firing me? I was too afraid to ask.

"You going to be all right, kid?"

"Yeah, of course. It's just one of those things, you know," I lied through my teeth.

Roger gave me a forceful pat on the shoulder and said he had to catch a flight back to LA, as if I didn't know he was a busy man. Roger was right about one thing though: I *had* always dreamed of changing the world. Who wants to flip on the news every night and see all the creative ways people can be horrible to one another? At the same time, I was losing hope that I could ever do a thing about it.

After all, I wasn't much of a hero.

CHAPTER

2

I stepped outside the theater and onto the street, where an icy wind punched me in the face. It was December in Chicago and that meant dealing with the elements. Northern winters look great on film, but safely negotiating snow-capped streets is tedious.

While my car warmed up, I stood under an old gas-lamp streetlight and watched drifting snow kiss wet pavement. A street saxophonist shared the corner with me, belting out Van Morrison's *There Will be Days Like This*. The fragrant aroma of roasting peanuts and boiled hot dogs filled my senses as one of those urban food carts rolled past. I looked around and saw couples holding hands and being cute together. Snow-covered city folk laughed with their friends and strolled about, happy as punch. It made me angry to see them so happy and carefree. Was I the only guy in the city whose dreams were collapsing around him? Was I the only one this… lonely?

A chilly wind pinched my bare skin, so I stepped over the sidewalk grates and let warm gutter steam blow up through the bottom of my pant-legs to reduce the numbness. I tried to spend as much time here as possible. Chicago, I mean—not standing over sidewalk vents. This is where I grew up and went to college. It had roots, and I was glad to be back for a while; maybe a long while. Most of my time was spent commuting to LA for meetings, which is a huge chore, but I couldn't stand the five years I lived out there. Andy Warhol once said, "I love Hollywood… everybody's plastic, but I love plastic."

Not me. Not any more.

Even as a young man, I knew that money wouldn't buy happiness but figured it would at least buy peace of mind. But now, just a bit wiser, I saw that money solved some problems while inventing new ones. I no longer had to worry about paying my bills, only to forgo the luxury of knowing if a girl was interested in me or my Lexus. With money and prestige comes a lack of trust. I trusted no one and that's the price you pay for success: loneliness. That's probably why I found myself giving that cute couple a dirty look. It's become a habit.

The drive home was a somber affair. It was just a few weeks until Christmas so holiday lights and tinsel were strewn across every streetlight and storefront window. It should have been a festive time of year, but not for me. The way things were turning out, I was quickly becoming a Scrooge.

Around 9 pm the snow flurries started to pick up, so I pulled over and ducked into a hole-in-the-wall Chinese restaurant to settle a stomach that was still in knots from the screening. I ordered a plate of fried noodles with sesame chicken and sat down in a booth by the window, wondering if such items exist on any menu in China. The owners of this joint aren't big on running the heat, even in the dead of winter, so I was glad to have brought a scarf with me. I began to miss LA's mild weather as I saw my breath form clouds between bites.

The door jingled and I looked up to see a young couple, probably in their twenties, bundled up and blowing into their hands to stay warm. They ordered some cashew chicken to go and then sat down at the table beside my booth while it was being prepared. They were another adorable couple, so naturally I had to choke back the rising vomit in my throat. After a few touch-and-go seconds, I was able to regain control of my diaphragm.

There's something I like to do when I'm in public, even though it's not entirely honest. I pretend I'm renting a movie and then ask random people what they think of one that I've actually produced. It's one of the few ways to get my finger on the pulse of an audience and since they don't have a clue who I am, the answers tend to be honest.

"Excuse me," I said to the guy. "I don't mean to bother you but my girlfriend sent me out to rent a movie and I'm not sure what to get. Have you guys seen *Dancing in the Meadows*?"

"Nope. Haven't seen it."

"What about *Danger Lives Here*?"

The girl turned toward me.

"Oh, I saw that one—isn't that where the gardener kills some woman's son and. . ."

"Daughter," I said, interrupting her with too much information. My cover was blown.

She gave me a funny look.

"I mean, I saw the trailer and I *think* it was the daughter," I mumbled.

"Oh," she replied. "Well, save your money. It sucks donkey balls."

I nodded politely. At least, I think I did. After stuffing my belly and starving my ego, I jumped back into the car and let the wipers knock an inch of dust off the windshield. I fired up the engine and headed onto the darkened streets. I was still thinking about the screening and what Roger had said to me. My thoughts were so jumbled that I missed my exit and ended up looping around to the west. In order to regain my bearings, I just took the first exit I saw and merged into a sea of taillights.

Fantastic!

The only thing worse than getting lost is getting lost *and* stuck in construction traffic. It was a two-lane road so I looked over to my right to see if I could get over. There was a small opening and I tried to merge, only to be blocked by a teenage girl chatting it up on her cell phone. I began motioning to her with my arm, asking for permission. She never even saw me.

I saw another opening and started to go. Just then, the car behind me sped up and jumped in to take the opening. Now I couldn't make the turn back onto the interstate; I was sure of it. I fumbled with my built-in GPS navigation, which shot back a warning.

"This feature has been disabled while the vehicle is moving. Please disengage…"

I hit the CANCEL button and nearly slammed into the back of the car in front of me. The guy gave me an *I'm going to kill you if you do that again* kind of glare.

"Be careful, old boy—watch the road," I said to myself while dreaming of a life without traffic jams and road rage.

I ended up missing the turn so I kept driving straight and eventually passed the bulk of construction traffic. I was now, however, hopelessly lost and the neighborhoods were looking less and less friendly.

"Why do I have to be in a nice car?" I thought to myself while passing some homeless men burning newspapers in a trash can. I looked at my watch. It was a little after 10 pm.

Suddenly I slammed on my brakes and came to a sliding halt. A woman in a heavy coat pushed a rusty shopping cart full of her possessions across the street and didn't seem to notice me.

"How can we live in a society where a person has to live that way?" I thought with a bit of shame on my conscience.

It was bone-chilling cold outside and this woman had no place to rest her head. I pulled alongside her, not knowing what to say.

"Excuse me, ma'am," I said out the window. Even rolling down the window sent chills all over my body on such a cold night.

The woman stopped and turned toward me, although her eyes looked past mine. I thought that perhaps she was blind.

"Do you have a place to stay tonight?"

She shook her head "no."

I wasn't even sure why I'd asked the question or what I planned on doing about it. I thought about maybe giving her a ride, but to where? I thought about taking her back to my house and letting her sleep in a warm place for a change. My eyes went down to her shopping cart, filled with the useless junk she called her only possessions.

Just then, I heard a loud thump and looked in my side view mirror. The two men I'd passed previously came up from the rear and one of them kicked my back bumper. They didn't look too welcoming, to say the least.

"You find some hookers someplace else. Leave that girl alone, you bitch ass punk!"

"I'm not looking for…" was all I got out of my mouth before he dented my door with an icy kick.

I gave the woman a look that said, "I'm sorry" and hit the gas pedal, speeding out of there with a slushy squeal. I looked back to see the two men shouting obscenities in my direction. It took a few minutes to realize that I could've been killed.

"The world can be a scary place when we misjudge the intentions of others," my father used to say.

I filed that thought away and looked for an interstate sign. I ended up driving all the way through the downtown area again before picking up the interstate on the other side of town. That was a long, one-hour detour that I didn't need. My eyes were heavy and I had to fight to stay conscious. At least I'll be able to sleep tonight, I thought to comfort myself. Lately, I'd only been able to sleep after a few glasses of wine, but that kind of self-medication can lead to worse problems than insomnia.

Twenty minutes later I pulled up to my neighborhood community and watched the gates slowly fold open with a metallic creak. I had only left twelve hours ago but it seemed like a week. My home was a sanctuary from the world of angry bosses and homeless guys wanting to kick my face in. It was the one place I didn't feel as lonely in the world.

I pulled into my circular driveway and cut the engine off. I sat there for a moment, just looking at my home. Most people would call it a mansion but it was a mid-sized property in this neighborhood. I sat in a Lexus in front of a 6,000-square-foot house and I had paid for none of it.

When you're broke, you can't catch a break. When you're rich, people give you everything for free. Both the house and the car were given to me as perks from the studio after my first three films brought in high box office numbers. I was pretty sure they couldn't take the house and car back now, but I still wondered. Nothing was certain on this hamster wheel of life that I knew. I feared being poor and having to work at McDonalds after tasting the good life; only I wasn't sure how "good" the good life was any more. Some days I wanted to run away, like a child escaping from an abusive home. I felt trapped. I hated the stress of always having to perform for a tyrannical boss and being stuck in a system that left me sleepless for nights on end. There wasn't a grain of integrity in this business and the feeling that no one actually cares about you can weigh on a person's soul.

I walked inside and smelled vanilla. "Must've left a candle burning again," I thought. I flipped on a light in the restroom and blew out a weak stem. Then I splashed some water on my face and stared at my sad reflection in the mirror. The person looking back at me was pale, with dark circles looming under tired eyes.

Inside the medicine cabinet I found some aspirin, which went down great with a glass of red wine. The evening's events had left me restless and sleep was evasive once more. I couldn't find the off switch to my brain, which kept me tossing and turning under silk sheets until I saw sunlight peeking through the blinds. I glanced at my clock and saw that it was five in the morning; I hadn't slept a wink. My coffee pot was on a timer so the aroma of Starbucks Christmas Blend began to waft into the bedroom. When the smell of coffee fills the house I might as well forget about getting any sleep. So I got up and slammed down two cups with a Pop Tart. Nothing like caffeine and high-fructose corn syrup to get your day started.

After a quick shower, I stood in my wardrobe and straightened a designer tie around my neck. I took one more look into the mirror and felt intense loneliness. During times like this, all I wanted was to turn around and have a supportive woman lovingly look at me and say, "You look marvelous, honey. Like a million bucks!" But I feared I would never be a part of one of those annoying cute couples. Some things were not meant to be. I took a troubled breath and felt a wave of shame and embarrassment pouring over me like a tsunami of failure.

But it wasn't the first time.

CHAPTER

3

The first time I fell in love, I was in the fifth grade. Heather was an older woman, at twelve, but she was the first to steal my heart. During lunch break I decided to stand up to a bully in order to earn a few social points, but the encounter resulted in me getting hit with a tray full of corn and body-slammed onto the tile floor in front of my peers. Teachers rushed over to break up the ruckus and I looked up and saw Heather wearing a face full of concern. We had never spoken, even once, but at that moment I knew she was the one for me.

After lunch we had gym class together and I decided to man up and take the seat beside Heather on the bleachers. She was sitting with Stephanie, a solid loaf who hated anything she couldn't eat, so this was going to be a challenge.

I opened with my best line, "Dodgeball is so awesome."

Heather looked me up and down, and then said, "Um, Ted… you're sweaty," at which point Stephanie chimed in with, "Yeah, and you smell like corn."

After the two of them chuckled and slapped one another high-five it became clear that my relationship with Heather wasn't working out. Heartbroken, but still a man of integrity, I decided to let her down gently.

"Heather, I wish you the best in life and hope you find whatever happiness you're looking for."

I stood up with an air of profundity, took two steps, then tumbled down the bleachers and busted my nose on the basketball court. I must've lost a pint of blood that day but what's more, I lost my childhood innocence. It was then I learned a painful life lesson: the world is a cold place and the natural inclination of mankind is bent toward selfishness, envy and getting ahead at the expense of others.

Yes, I was a deep kid and read too much into things. Even still, my conclusion turned out right.

I sat in the nurse's office with gauze spun around my nose. I looked up at a world map on the wall and my eyes were drawn toward a long cluster of islands in the South China Sea. I reached out a bony finger and touched the map as the school nurse entered the room behind me.

She noticed my curiosity and said, "Making some travel plans, are we?"

She offered me a warm smile and I nodded in response. "Yeah, one day I'm going to disappear to a place where no one can find me."

"I see you've chosen the Philippines. You know, I heard there's thousands of tiny islands over there. I bet you could still grab one or two of them if you had the money."

"I'll never have that kind of money."

She looked at me with curious eyes and said, "I guess you'd better get used to bloody noses then."

She gave a gentle smile but I knew she was right. My mother had died the year before and it was times like this when I needed a mom to hug me and tell me the lie every kid wants to hear: *it'll be all right.*

My father did his best in a tough situation but was, despite all efforts, a complete dork—a trait passed on to me without having evolved much. Pops never quite knew what was "cool" but liked to think he was up to speed, even though he was always a couple of years behind the pack. I still remember that Christmas following Mom's death. It was a sad time for both Pops and me but he was especially excited about a big surprise gift he'd picked out that year. After dropping a few hints, I figured out that he'd gotten me the newly released—and very popular among my peers—Nintendo Entertainment System. It was all the rage and you were not cool in 1985 unless you had a Nintendo. People at school would trade games and talk about all their codes and tricks to beat difficult levels. I wanted in on that crowd like you wouldn't believe.

So when Pops, giddy with excitement, handed me a heavy, poorly wrapped box, I was about to jump out of my skin with excitement! As I started tearing into my present, he suddenly stopped me, ran into the next room to fetch his Polaroid camera, then came back and centered me in the frame before saying, "It's okay—go ahead and open it now."

I tore through the paper only to see a sad-looking Atari 5200. This game system had been out for around three years and by 1985 was the laughingstock of the gaming world. I was hurt and angry.

How could Pops not know how dorky this was? Didn't he understand that I couldn't swap games or make new friends with an Atari? Give me a break!

But then I saw the look on his face, full of enthusiasm and joy, and it softened me.

I gave him a big, fake hug and said, "Thanks, Dad. You're the best."

As we broke, I saw his eyes begin to water with joy and I felt at that moment I was a terrible son. Pops had done his best and I was an ungrateful brat. Of course, a few years later Dad bought me that Nintendo, but Sega was all the rage by that point. God bless his clueless soul.

CHAPTER

4

I ate my birthday dinner alone at an oversized family table in the den, watching *It's a Wonderful Life* while having overcooked salmon and Château Lafite. I fell asleep in the living room around ten-thirty and had a strange dream about my assistant, Teresa. She was a cute girl and a heck of a lot of fun to converse with, but I'd never thought about her in a romantic way. In the dream we were outside in a courtyard, which oddly resembled Mr. Miyagi's back yard from one of the *Karate Kid* sequels. It was snowing but didn't feel cold outside. We sat in the landscaped garden near a koi pond, eating chocolate-dipped strawberries and laughing. The only audible dialogue I remember was when Teresa leaned over and said, "I can't believe how good this feels."

Of course, I woke up severely in love with her. It's funny how that happens. The only thing I'd ever thought about Teresa prior to that dream was that she happened to be a snappy dresser. I mentioned this to her once so she got into the habit of calling me a metrosexual, a term which terribly offended me until I Googled it and found out it was sort of a compliment. She was 28 years old but might as well have been 15 because I couldn't understand most of what she said. Teresa liked to stay current and her lingo was very hip, making me feel like a dinosaur in my mid-thirties.

I walked into the kitchen to grab some coffee and saw that I had a missed call. Speak of the devil. It's not rare to get a call from Teresa since she *is* my assistant, but the timing made things weird. I fought off the urge to call her back right away but there was a chance she had important news.

"It was just a dream," I told myself. "If you were in love with her it would have become obvious during the two years she's worked for you, and not just after a dream in which she said something cute while we shared strawberries."

What was it she said again? I *can't believe how good this feels.*

I let that thought linger a little too long and found myself dialing her number.

"Hello?" said the love of my life.

"Teresa, hi, it's Ted. I saw that you'd called."

"Ted, hey—you sound weird. You all right?"

"Weird? You're weird. What do you mean?"

"Oh, never mind—it must be the connection. So I just wanted to remind you about the speaking gig at NYU next month. I know how you like to put things off to the last minute so…"

"Can we cancel that one? Is it too late?"

"Well, you know Jerry will kill you, right?"

"Yes, I know he'll throw a hissy. Then he'll get over it like he always does."

"Why don't I give you a few days to think it over?" she said.

The fact that she knew me so well made her all the more adorable.

"Anything from Roger?" I asked, fearing the answer already.

"Yep, that's actually the reason I called…"

Then she paused; I knew something was up.

"Do you want me to do this over the phone?" she asked.

"Just give it to me straight. What's the word?"

What's the word? Who was I, The Fonz?

She paused again and said, "He wants you to supervise the Maynard film. They're having some issues."

This was worse than getting fired. It was like being sent to purgatory. I forgot to respond.

"You okay?" she asked, genuinely concerned.

"No, yeah—I'm fine."

"He said it was because you're the only man for the job. And also because they're shooting in Grant Park and you're already in town."

"I got it. No biggie, right? At least we still have a paycheck."

"That's the spirit!" she enthused.

"Okay, then—well, thanks for giving me the news."

"That's why I'm here, TL."

"Thanks, Teresa. I love…"

Uh oh.

"What's that? Ted… are you still there? I think our connection is jacked."

My brain was reeling. *Think fast!*

"I mean, tell Roger I'd love to work on the project and thank him for giving me something close to home for a change."

"Coolio. Hit me back if you need me for anything."

"I will. Bye now."

"Lates," she said in a perky voice.

My assignment was to supervise a train wreck of a film called *Gypsy Girl.* Two years ago my name was inked in the trades, an amalgamation that refers to *The Hollywood Reporter* and *Variety* magazines, for producing the two biggest hits of the summer. Now Roger was sending me out here to salvage a crumbling production with a hothead director and a team that couldn't manage a lemonade stand. They were two million over budget and the director threatened to quit every other day. Frankly, I wished that he would.

• • •

The next day I showed up on set bright and early, hoping for the best. We were already an hour behind schedule when the generator went down. By the time we got a replacement up and running our camera operator had managed to crack a seventy-five thousand dollar Panavision lens, resulting in a very fun phone conversation with the insurance company. It wasn't even lunchtime and I was already sweating bullets.

As I went to snatch a quick coffee, the lead actress approached me in a huff and yelled, "I can't work with that guy! He's an idiot!"

She pointed a finger at the director, who was watching us from a safe distance behind a row of production monitors. He returned the finger, his middle one, and then grabbed his crotch.

Wonderful.

"He's an eccentric guy. You just have to warm up to him a little."

"I'm calling my agent. Screw this."

"Whoa, whoa, whoa—that's not even necessary. Let me go have a chat with him."

Cory Maynard was the source of my current frustration. He was a UCLA film grad who'd won an MTV movie award for his last flick, a thought-provoking piece about a monkey who took a hit of acid and was then transformed into a genius, endearing him to the masses until he became the first chimp President of the United States. If you're wondering if the chimp President demanded to be paid in bananas, the answer is yes. Yes he did. And female monkeys.

I feel nauseous.

To put it mildly, Cory was not an easy guy to work with. Roger picked him because he was called "the next big thing" by a major film publication and the press loved him since he gave them plenty of material about which to write. I approached Cory with a diplomatic producer's grin. Total cheese.

"Cory, my man. What do you say we don't make the lead actress quit three weeks into production and lose forty million dollars?"

"Ted, you know exactly nothing. That chick is a spoiled brat."

"Oh, the irony," I thought.

"Cory, we can't replace her this late into the schedule. Roger will murder both of us. And that's not a figure of speech."

Roger's name sobered him up fast. He fell silent and looked at the floor. Sometimes I felt like producing a movie was very much akin to babysitting four-year-olds.

"I'll make you a deal," I said. "Cut the crap and apologize and I'll put some points into your contract."

"How many?"

"More than the zero you have now. Can you keep the peace on my set?"

Cory sighed into my face so hard I felt his breath on my forehead.

"Fine," he said with a note of reluctance.

He then gave a model's turn as if rounding the catwalk, and returned to his post. One more fire had been extinguished, but I knew it would not be the last.

CHAPTER

5

I met Jerry, my manager, at our usual spot for dinner. He was a short, impatient man in his early fifties who liked to smoke weed and party with girls half his age. Jerry wore thousand dollar suits and always smelled like he'd just had a bath in after-shave. He might have been a creep but he always got me a fair salary from Roger, so I kept him around.

There was some chatter in the room as I scanned the menu for new items. Jerry was busy squeezing lemon into his water, which he insisted on stirring with his index finger. I always found his mannerisms disgusting. My mood was especially sour since I wasn't sure if I'd be able to get *Gypsy Girl* back on track. Roger Graham didn't appreciate failure so my neck was on the line in a big way.

Teresa entered my mind again. I wondered what kinds of things bothered her. Did *anything* bother her? She was always so upbeat and positive.

I noticed Jerry looking at me funny. We had hardly spoken since we sat down so I decided to engage.

"Negotiating traffic in this town is bordering on suicide. I'm going back to cabs."

"You think cabs are safer?"

"Are you happy with your life?" I blurted out, already tired of small talk. "I mean… genuinely happy?"

He paused for a moment to think about it and said, "Yeah. I guess so."

"You're lying. You can't be happy. Do you even know what goes on in the world?"

He looked at me with sincere eyes and said, "What is it with you? Why does every conversation turn into some rant against corporate greed or starving orphans? Can't we just be two guys enjoying a meal for once?"

"I'm in love with Teresa," I said, getting to the point.

"No you're not."

"I had a dream about her and I woke up in love. I thought it would go away but it's been a week and I still feel this weird affection for her."

"Ted, listen—don't ever fall for your assistant. Especially Teresa. You two have nothing in common outside of work. If you want some chicks to party with, say the word."

"I know. She'd never go for me anyway," I thought out loud. "Girls like that are always swooning over some jerk who drives a Harley and gives them a black eye for putting cold soup on the table."

"You're doing the talk next month, right?"

Jerry kept setting up these speaking engagements for me because they earned him a small commission but he knew how much I hated public speaking. He didn't care; the guy was a shark. Unfortunately, he was also the only friend I had.

"Yeah... I'm doing the speech. But this is the last one. You know I hate doing those."

Jerry smiled as he turned his attention back to the menu. He always won.

"Did you know they have clams now?"

My mind revolted.

"I don't eat mollusks, Jerry. You're aware of the term *bottom feeder*?"

He looked at me with pity.

"What?" I said innocently enough.

"Ted, you're going to die of worry one day."

• • •

The next day I stepped onto the set with a slight cold, glad that we only had a week left until wrap. I'd spent the last nine days outside in the cold, fighting off a runny nose and a strong temptation to murder Cory Maynard. It was a Thursday morning and the wind coming off Lake Michigan was especially chilly. We had to get two major scenes done by two o'clock in order to stay on budget and make our day. If you didn't get all your shots for the day, it meant paying overtime to the entire crew, as well as the actors—who were already paid too much to begin with. A production assistant walked over to me, blowing warm air into his mitts.

"Cory won't come out of his trailer," was all he said.

I didn't even feel like asking. This guy was about to get on my last nerve.

I stormed over to his trailer and pounded my fist against the door. When he didn't respond, I kicked the door as hard as I could, almost falling on my ass. Finally, the door swung open and Cory appeared in the doorway with glazed eyes. He was a mess.

"Call time was seven fifteen!" I shouted. "If we go into overtime today, guess whose paycheck that's coming out of. That would be YOURS!"

Cory stumbled back, grabbing the wall to steady himself. He then looked at me with sad eyes and began to cry. A dozen beer cans were strewn behind him.

Lord… take me now, I prayed in my head.

"Cory, what's going on? What is this about?"

He used his sleeve to wipe a mixture of tears and snot from his face.

"Ginger left me," he said, sobbing so heavily that he sounded like a teenage girl after her first break-up.

But for the first time in my life, I actually felt some kind of sympathy for the spoiled brat. I sat down next to him inside the trailer, trying to think of something to say. I began to put my arm around him but decided against it since I might be tempted to choke him with it. Instead, I looked down at my watch to see that we were quickly losing the day.

"Cory, look… I know you and Ginger had a special thing going. She was a great girl, especially after she got out of rehab that second time. I've been heartbroken more than a few times myself and you know what? The best thing to do is to stay busy."

"Seriously?" he asked, slobbering all over himself.

"Distraction is a wonderful thing. And besides, you're a professional, Cory. The best there is! If a no-talent idiot like me can put his personal life aside and get on with his work, how much more can a guy like you?"

When you deal with Hollywood types and you're out of resources, you must resort to stroking their egos. It'll get you more mileage than logic and reason ever will. Cory freshened up and went onto the set a new man. He took command, acted his age, and got us in on schedule. And I couldn't have been happier.

CHAPTER

6

My time in purgatory was almost up. Roger called me to say thanks for getting *Gypsy Girl* to the finish line. He admitted that the assignment was a test to see if I still had the goods and was happy to know that I might be ready for the big leagues again. However, Roger wanted to give me one final test, and this was a big one.

I sat down that evening with the distinguished Richard Crowntree, Chicago native and screenwriter extraordinaire. Being a man of simple tastes and not recognizing a thing on the menu, I ordered a French-sounding dish with a poorly imitated accent. Social situations always bothered me, especially when I had a goal in mind. It made me feel like a car salesman.

Richard was a respected man, and for good reason. He'd written thirteen studio films and none of them had lost money. That kind of track record is quite the gem in this industry. Roger Graham had given me one objective for this meeting: make Richard sign a contract to write our next film. There was also a veiled threat about my career hinging on the success of this meeting. It should be mentioned that when Roger fires a person, getting another job in the entertainment business is next to impossible. So you'd better have a back-up plan.

I looked at him and said, "Richard, I'd like you to write our next picture. Mr. Graham is ready to offer seven figures up front with a completion bonus, first re-write clause and points on the back end."

I finished my pitch, short and sweet, and waited for his reaction. Richard was busy folding a knot into his napkin.

"You ever wonder what makes people tick, Ted?"

As a film producer, I'd grown accustomed to comments coming out of left field when trying to close a deal. But I really needed a solid "yes" here and I wasn't willing to follow Richard Crowntree down this trail.

"I certainly do. It's my business to know how people tick; otherwise I'd never get them to fill theater seats."

"I think about it a lot," he said. "As a writer I have to confront that issue head on, day in and day out and I must do so with great honesty and introspection."

I had to defuse this slumber party quickly.

"And that's what makes you so special, Richard. You really understand human nature and that totally comes through in your work. Audiences get that about you. Did I mention the first re-write clause?"

Richard swirled red wine around his glass and took a sip. I needed him to stay with me but his eyes were increasingly distant.

"You know," he said in a soft tone. "I saw a news report last week where a man broke into his ex-girlfriend's house, shot her daughter to death and then lit the woman on fire. Afterward there was a police shoot-out and an officer was killed."

"Yeah, I saw that too," was all I could muster.

"It got me thinking, you know… if human beings can do such horrible things to each other, how decent would a person have to be in order to shift the scales back to zero?"

I was not exactly following Richard's train of thought but he obviously wanted to get something off his chest, so I fell silent.

"I don't see how people like us can sit back and make movies while the world implodes. Some say there's benefit to entertaining the masses, to keep their spirits up and whatnot. But I wonder… I really wonder how much good it does. I doubt the wife of that police officer who was killed last week will be comforted by any of the crap I, or anyone else, has written. I am seriously at my wits' end here. Turn on the news… all you see is violence and anger and hatred—it never ends. I'm sitting here drinking wine, about to eat a seventy-five dollar steak, and there's a widow at home on the South Side of Chicago with three kids and a stack of bills, all because some idiot lost his temper and started spraying bullets at people who took an oath to protect the innocent and serve their community. How is that fair, Ted? How can we look at ourselves in the mirror?"

He let the question linger but I wasn't sure he wanted an answer.

I began slowly, "Richard, we all have these thoughts and to be honest, it gets to me too. I sometimes feel like even my most inspiring work is like giving a band-aid to a cancer patient. I feel where you're coming from. Yes, people do terrible things, but there's also good in the world. A positive film can remind people of that... give them perspective, give them hope. That widow on the South Side ... maybe we tell her story. We show the world what true bravery is and perhaps inspire some kind of healing. You write that story, Richard, and let me cast it. She'll get a nice paycheck to satisfy her pile of bills and we'll both be doing something that matters. No, it won't rid the world of evil, but things will be a little bit better because of us... because of your decision to say 'yes' and sign this contract."

I couldn't believe what was coming out of my mouth—a movie about a slain police officer and his widow? That was not the kind of blockbuster Roger Graham had in mind. In fact, it was tantamount to box office suicide. Hopefully my words rang empty with Richard and he'd go on about his seventy-five dollar steak. Much to my dismay, his eyes perked up.

Uh oh, he was genuinely interested.

Richard straightened in his seat. "Ted, that's brilliant! This is my swan song. I'll write a film that will change lives and I don't care if it makes money or not!"

"Whoa there, let's not get too excited," I cautioned. "I have to run this past Roger, of course."

I was no longer in the room as far as Richard Crowntree was concerned. I was a vanishing muse, not worthy of eye contact. He looked out into some distant realm as a smile stretched across his face. A few moments later Richard borrowed a pen from the waiter and put his signature on the dotted line. I was both happy and grieved, wondering how Roger would take the news:

Congratulations, we got Richard Crowntree to write our next movie but it's the kind of story that won't sell five tickets!

This was all starting to look grim. When I got home that night, I stretched out on my leather sofa and began to contemplate what had transpired over dinner. Was my advice to make this film actually sound? Could it work? And even if it resulted in a commercial flop and my career was ruined, at least that poor widow would be able to pay off her mortgage from the story rights. I was beginning to feel like it was the right decision. To help a family that genuinely deserved it made me feel warm inside, and that was not a common occurrence.

CHAPTER

7

The flight from Chicago to LA only takes four hours but it seemed like an eternity because I was flying in for a closed-door meeting with Roger Graham, the kind of meeting they'd likely tell stories about after scraping my body off of some random sidewalk. I spent the whole time thinking about how I was going to convince him to greenlight the project Richard and I came up with in our moment of exuberance.

The deck was stacked against me but, like in Vegas, there's always a chance. I would start by talking to Roger about what got us into the movie business in the first place, our passion for great storytelling. That will soften him up a bit and I'll then slide in with the current news stories and how we might be able to use our craft for the good of mankind. I even heard thunderous applause in my head. By the time we landed at LAX, I had already convinced myself that I could get him to make this film. And that was just the momentum I needed.

• • •

Roger didn't even look up from his copy of Variety when I walked in.

"Don't sit down; this won't take long," he said as he sipped his coffee. His office always smelled like cigar smoke and musk, with a dash of fear.

He continued, "We had the legal department dissolve Robert Crowntree's contract yesterday."

"What do you mean?"

"Come on... a sappy drama? There's no way we'd make a return on such drivel. You did a great job in getting him to sign, Teddy, but we're going to use Craig Fleishman instead. He's going to write an end-of-the-world epic with aliens."

I paused briefly, choking on my own saliva, and spoke up. "Why don't we do them both? Surely we can get Robert's drama greenlit too."

"What's wrong with you? The money people are scared: only big franchise films from now on. Let the Weinstein's make that garbage. We already had this talk if you don't remember."

I was desperate, and already walking a thin line.

"Robert's film will get you that Oscar you've been swooning over. Think about it. This alien picture, that'll put money in the bank but you and I are both wealthy men. What we don't have is an Oscar."

"Hey, idiot. Hey… LOOK AT ME! I'M TIRED OF EXPLAINING THIS TO YOU ALL THE TIME! WHAT DON'T YOU UNDERSTAND?"

My pulse hit a thousand beats a minute. Roger had never yelled at me before like this. I took a few quick breaths.

"You're right," I said. "I'm sorry. I just thought…"

"That we could change things?" he said, finishing my sentence. "Right, Teddy? That's what you want—change? I can certainly make some changes around here if that's what you want. There's a million people who would kill to have your job."

The word *kill* made me nervous but I'd never forgive myself if I turned into a coward at this moment. I owed it to Richard Crowntree. I owed it to that police officer's wife.

"I can take losing my job, Roger. But I can't take losing my soul. We should do the right thing."

"What?" He physically pulled his face back. "Is there a hidden camera in here? Is this a joke?"

"It'll make money. Trust me. I believe in this project. Richard has never written a flop."

"If you want to make a picture about some ghetto bitch in the slums then be my guest. But you won't be doing it with our money."

I was actually shocked by his callous tone.

"Why did you get into this business, Roger? I thought you wanted to…"

"Look, Ted, I'm not taking this stroll down memory lane with you. I'm a pragmatic guy. I do what works. I suggest you follow suit unless you want to be begging for change out on the sidewalk in a month."

"I'm not afraid of you," I said in a thin voice that proved I was.

"Ted, you're lucky that you're more valuable to me alive than dead."

"We should make this movie, Roger."

He shook his head and did something I never would have expected: he smiled. It was subtle but it was definitely a smile.

He looked up and said, "You got guts, Teddy. And I'd be lying if I said I didn't respect you for it. You talk a good game."

I started to loosen up.

"But the answer is no. End of discussion."

At that moment I knew it wasn't going to happen. There was nothing I could've said to change his mind. And it made me sick. The only thing I could see was that poor woman, her fatherless children and a stack of unpaid bills. Oh, and seventy-five dollar steak.

I excused myself into the hallway, where I began to dry heave while racing toward the restroom. I somehow managed to lock the door before turning around and blasting the room with projectile vomit.

After lying on the cold tile for what seemed like twenty minutes, and ignoring multiple knocks on the door, I was able to pry myself up using the sink for balance. I stood in front of the mirror, looking at a splendidly dressed man in a fifteen-hundred-dollar suit and five-hundred-dollar shoes, covered in guilt-induced puke. What a bizarre and ironic sight.

The next day I flew back to Chicago. My car pulled into the neighborhood around nightfall and the gates opened more slowly than usual. Even they were tired. After freshening up with a shower and change of clothes, I broke open the laptop and spent nearly an hour on Google, looking for an address. I'm quite savvy with the search engines and even then I had to progress down a number of dead ends before hitting the jackpot.

I rolled up in front of Delores Jackson's home around seven fifteen. It was a charming but aged brownstone. As I stepped out of the car, the smell of cardboard and burning wood suddenly congested my nostrils. Tinsel and cheap Christmas lights dangled from metal railing. There were two men drinking out of paper sacks at the end of the street, both of whom were eyeballing me suspiciously. They must've pegged me as a landlord, what with the car and all. I smiled and waved but was met with blank stares.

I walked up the steps, the muted sound of children crying not far away. I knocked on the heavy door, held in place by a dilapidated frame and, probably, cobwebs. I heard Delores trying to quiet her kids, maybe a gesture of respect, before swinging the door open.

"Delores Jackson?"

She was a pretty, slender African-American woman in her early thirties or late twenties. She immediately wiped her hair to the side, which I assumed was a panicked attempt to freshen up for company. It was charming.

"Can I help you?"

"I heard about your situation," was the first thing I could muster. "I guess everyone did."

I've never been good at the opening line. There was a long pause and she looked at me with glimmering eyes, filled with youth and questions.

"May I come in?"

"Uh… oh. I'm not sure. Who…?"

"Right. You have no idea who I am."

Thinking quickly, I fished around in my wallet and pulled out a business card, which I handed to her.

She took the card, glanced over it.

"What's an executive producer?"

"I oversee movie productions and deal with project financing. Not so much a creative job these days, but I…"

"And why did you come here again? I'm certainly not an actress."

"Of course. Well, I wanted to meet you and say that I'm sorry for your loss. And because I may be able to help your children. And you."

That felt rushed, and too soon. Delores hesitated, eyes dropping to the business card once more. She took a minute to think it over, then stepped back and showed me in. The house was a wreck, no doubt the result of losing a husband and facing the sobering thought of having to raise two young children, all in the span of three weeks. But even so, I could see that she was trying.

An older woman took the kids into the living room as Delores showed me a faded yellow kitchen with old, stained appliances from the 70s. A frying pot sat on a burner with old grease inside, the smell of which made my stomach queasy.

The whole apartment felt chilly so I bundled my coat and scarf tighter, then noticed that Delores was barefoot.

A few Hallmark cards lined her refrigerator, along with a crayon drawing of a tall man in police uniform with a big red heart around him. Written at the bottom of the page were the words:

Miss you daddy! Sleep tight!

Chills shot up my arms. What in the hell was I doing here? I didn't know these people. This wasn't my life. Her husband was dead, rotting away under a mound of dirt and

I was standing here in the middle of all this madness, pretending I could actually do something for these people. I panicked, my eyes searching around for an exit.

Delores, who was observing me carefully, was even more confused than before. She eased me into a chair like a nurturing mother whose child had just skinned a knee.

"Sir, would you like something to drink? I have… well… water. But I can go to the store if you'd prefer something with more flavor."

"No, I'm fine, but thanks."

"Were you a friend of Eddie's?" She asked.

"I didn't know your husband, Mrs. Jackson. I just came here because I wanted to talk to you. You see, I might be able to… improve your situation."

"Have we met?" she asked curiously.

"No." I sucked in a breath. "But my parents died when I was fairly young and they had set up this trust fund which allowed me to go through school and not have to worry about paying for rent or groceries. That trust fund wasn't able to bring my parents back to life but it helped me attain a certain position in life. And that's the reason I'm here tonight. I know you're going to think I'm crazy and what I'm about to do will in no sense bring your husband back or change the pain in your heart but…"

I took out my checkbook and tore off a pre-written check for one hundred thousand dollars. Who knows why I chose that amount but it seemed a good, round figure. I passed the check to her quivering hand and felt a heavy weight dislodge from my shoulders. There was a moment of disbelief in her eyes. She covered her mouth and tried to speak.

"Why are you doing this?" she sobbed.

"Because I'm able to."

"But why me? There's a million people in this city and at least a dozen on this block who could use this more than me. I don't deserve this."

"I have my convictions so let's please leave it at that. I need you to deposit this into your account first thing in the morning. The bank will require you to go through a mediator due to the large sum. That's perfectly normal; they aren't trying to scam you. Just sign the legal documents they present to you and have them call my office to verify that the funds are available. You have my card."

Delores looked at me like I was a life raft in the middle of the ocean but I was strangely beginning to feel the same way toward her. She nodded her head while smiling through tears.

"Your name is Ted?" she inquired.

"Yes. Theodore Preston LaSalle."

"That's a good name. From now on that name will be held in the highest regard in my family. I'm going to hug everyone I meet named Ted."

"Yeah, be careful with that kind of affection—you're a pretty happening chick."

Happening chick?

I didn't expect to be hit with such a flurry of emotions and had no time to react. The smelly kitchen and cold, cluttered apartment sent me into uncharted emotional waters. And the crushing weight of loneliness had fallen to the floor with a loud thud. I'd found a friend.

We both smiled and laughed. I spent another couple of hours with Delores and her kids, not wanting it to end. She told me they had been praying for something to happen since her husband's life insurance wasn't enough to get them through financially. They walked me to my car and saw me off with tears of joy, much to the bewilderment of the gentlemen still standing on the corner. I felt a strange sense of family being around Delores and her kids and by the way she welcomed me into her home.

And then, on the drive home, I wondered why I hadn't given her more.

Just a couple of weeks earlier, her story broke on the evening news and it threw acclaimed screenwriter, Richard Crowntree, into a world of desperation and hopelessness. But despite the way things went down with the film, something truly good came out of this and Richard would be proud, though I'd never tell him what I had done. My father used to tell me: *To boast is to invite calamity to your front porch.* Pops knew what he was talking about.

CHAPTER

8

Looking out over the city from my office, I contemplated the next move. Things were dicey with Roger but something had occurred to me over the course of the past few weeks: I no longer enjoyed producing movies. I got into this business because I had an overpowering desire to create stories that last—the kind that change people. I wanted a life that didn't involve tiptoeing around Roger Graham. What I wanted, in reality, was freedom.

I installed some screenwriting software on my office computer and started out with a simple opening. They say to write what you know.

FADE IN:
INT. OFFICE—DAY
A tall man with unkempt hair thought about asking out his assistant on a date. He was pensive.

There was a light knock on the door and Teresa entered my office wearing a well-matched skirt suit, carrying a stack of papers to my desk. I didn't want her to see what I was writing so instead of trying to swivel the monitor away, and look suspicious, my fingers hit the keyboard in a random fashion, typing a fake URL into the address bar. Much to my chagrin, a porn site popped up just as Teresa looked over. Ouch.

"Oh no… I must have typed in the wrong address—this is not my kind of thing," I said as my face turned three shades of red.

Teresa smiled politely.

"You don't have to explain."

She took my empty mug of coffee and walked toward the door. I didn't need a refill but it was too painful to speak at that moment.

And then something odd happened. Teresa stopped in front of the door and turned to me slowly with a worried, almost motherly, expression on her face.

"Ted," she said in a soft voice.

"What's up?"

"You should maybe get out, ya know?"

I looked at her, puzzled.

"Out? As in…?"

"Meet some people. Make some friends."

"Jerry's my friend."

"He's your agent. There's a difference."

I was beginning to sense that Teresa saw me as some kind of sappy loser with no knowledge of the social world. That would have been accurate but I needed cover.

"Hey, you know me by now. I'm a man who values his privacy. Some people need close friends or whatever to feel complete. I don't. My work is very fulfilling."

She quickly apologized, "I'm sorry. I didn't mean to pry. That was intrusive."

"No, it's okay," I said. "Some people just prefer to be alone in life. Loners, you know—like Michael Jackson. Not Michael Jackson. James Dean. He was a loner. I'm James Dean."

That was weak and she knew it. I was trying too hard to convince her that I preferred things the way they were.

"I just worry about you sometimes."

"Why would you worry about me?" I said, a little too enthusiastically.

"Well," she started. "I know things aren't going all that well with Roger. He's a bit of a nightmare to have to deal with. Having someone you can talk to about things—it really helps."

I felt the urge to ask her out but resisted. I had an extreme dislike for guys who hit on women who work for them. I just found it creepy and would prefer to drink boiling acid than have Teresa ever see *me* that way. So I let the moment pass and said, "Thanks, Teresa. You're right."

"Always am, Mr. Dean."

She smiled warmly and walked out.

• • •

My house seemed lonelier than ever that night. Even the perfectly chilled glass of Château Margaux and breezy notes of Tchaikovsky didn't lift my mood. Since the usual tricks were no longer working, I decided to take Teresa's advice and get out of the house. I needed to be around people.

On restless nights, I liked to take a boardwalk stroll down Navy Pier, which looks out over the vast waters of Lake Michigan. It provided a beautiful view of the Chicago skyline as well.

A light snow fell as I got to the Pier and only then noticed that it had been closed down for the evening.

"Where is everyone?" I thought to myself.

It was a rare occasion when I actually felt like being social, so what gives? I looked down at my watch and saw that it was a little past midnight. I then realized that it was a Wednesday evening and most people don't have the luxury of walking around at midnight during the week.

Although the chilly night air was beginning to pierce my lungs with each breath, I was mesmerized by the beauty around me. The wind blowing in from Lake Michigan created this gentle ballet of snowdrifts, prompting a rather dreamlike atmosphere. There I stood, among the shifting patterns of snow, illuminated by street lamps glowing overhead. It was pure bliss, and no one was around. I felt alone while surrounded by skyscrapers and the sensation of snowflakes hitting my skin.

That's when I heard the voice.

It was a woman's voice, faint in the distance. I couldn't see through the drifting snow but that sound was definitely human. I moved forward blindly, trying to discern its origin. As I moved closer and closer toward the source, I was able to make out the words.

"Help me!"

I ran as fast as I could toward the voice and through the thick snow I saw a woman being thrown to the ground by a large man. I ran so fast it felt like I was in warp-speed, kicking up a trail of white dust behind me.

I can't possibly be running this fast! I thought to myself while shooting toward the end of the street in this weird, hypnotic state. My heart was beating so fast it was all I could hear, besides the crunching snow under foot.

The guy looked up just as I smashed into him with a full-speed tackle! We immediately hit the ground and it felt like running head first into a brick wall. There was a flash of blackness and an intense pain between my eyes. My ears rang. I was dazed and couldn't find my balance. The focus in my eyes was all but lost.

For a moment I groped around, trying to regain my bearings. Where was I? Had I just tackled a fully grown man? A shooting pain went through my head, from ear to ear. I then caught a glimpse of the helpless woman, her right cheek swollen and red.

Suddenly, out of nowhere, I felt someone take hold of my waist and I was airborne. My feet were well above my head when I crashed down hard onto the icy sidewalk. The man jumped on top of me and I saw flashes of downward punches, muted sounds thumping my brain against the base of my skull. Over and over. I couldn't see.

I began to choke on the snow as it traveled down the back of my throat, mixed with the awful, metallic taste of blood.

"DO SOMETHING!" I said to myself. "DO SOMETHING BEFORE YOU GET KILLED!"

Although numb to the punches, I seriously thought I might suffocate from the snow collapsing into my face. It was terrifying not to see what was happening, even if the snow was buffering the punches a bit. Still dizzy and battered, I somehow managed to roll him off me. I got to my feet, head spinning and no sense of direction, and saw the man going once more for the woman I assumed was his girlfriend.

She shouted, "Stop it, Steven! Just stop it! Help me, please!"

I once more stumbled toward the man and latched onto him from behind in some sort of bear hug. We fell to the ground in such a way that I was able to wrap my forearm around his neck. I squeezed and squeezed with all my might with what felt like inhuman strength. I knew that choking him unconscious would allow me and the woman to flee to safety so there was no way I was letting go! The blood and tension rushing into my forearms caused them to cramp up. The pain was unbearable but I continued to squeeze.

Suddenly, I heard my voice involuntarily scream out in pain! It took a moment to realize what was happening. I felt a sharp, searing pain in my back and all my muscles locked up at once. I fell over onto my side, unable to move. The man got to his feet and I saw the woman I had rescued standing over me holding a large folding knife.

"Get his wallet! Hurry up!" she urged.

I felt paralyzed as I lay there in the snow with two strangers pilfering through my pockets. The woman grabbed my money clip, removed my cash, and tossed the clip back down onto my face. And then, in a flash, they were gone—and I was alone. I blinked once and then lost consciousness.

CHAPTER

9

Suddenly everything felt warm and when I opened my eyes the room was so bright it burned them. After a moment of adjustment, it became clear that I was in a hospital bed. A nurse poked her head into the room and when she saw that I was awake she smiled and moved toward me.

"Do you know where you are?" she asked.

"The Critical Care Unit of Mercy Hospital?"

She grinned and said, "That's a pretty good guess. But we've moved you out of Critical Care."

I saw that the woman looked Polynesian so I asked where she was from.

"I grew up in LA but I was born in the Philippines. Why do you ask?"

In a split second my mind traveled back to that fifth grade nurse's lounge and the map. I wanted to ask her if it was a nice place where people didn't stab you in the back—both literally and figuratively.

"You were on the news earlier," she said. "They did a quick piece on you but didn't give your name or anything. "

I began to say something and then passed out.

After a few hours of very bizarre dreams I woke up sweating. They must've given me some wicked drugs because I didn't feel a thing, not even a twinge of pain in my back. Everything was numb. I grabbed my cell phone from the little plastic tray beside the bed and flipped it open. There was not a single missed call. I was disappointed for a second, and then realized nobody had a clue what had happened to me.

I flipped on the small TV that was mounted on the wall, a far cry from the type of set-up I had back home. I found a local news station and nearly jumped out of bed when I saw a familiar face!

Delores Jackson's profile was on the screen as a reporter informed us of breaking news. I couldn't help but wonder if the press had discovered our little secret but I was hoping to keep her out of the limelight, for the sake of her kids. I also hoped Delores had not seen me on the news because she'd be scared out of her wits.

"The thirty-one year old Jackson, whose police officer husband was shot to death recently while on duty, was driving erratically last evening when police tried to pull her over. Not responding, the state trooper shot out her back tires and the car flipped and then slammed into a tree, killing her instantly. Friends of Jackson say she had a history of epilepsy. A toxicology report will determine whether or not alcohol was involved in the incident but friends of the family tell us she was not a drinker."

I just stared at the television as they moved on to the next story. This wasn't real. It was the drugs they'd given me. That's it. This wasn't real. Just a hallucination brought on by mild opiates. There's no way…

I tried to talk, just to hear someone's voice, but only a deep groan came out. I began to sob in a manner that I had not known before and the moment overtook me. Feeling I had no control whatsoever, I chucked the remote at the TV and shattered the screen!

A couple of nurses ran into the room, thinking I had hurt myself. Still in a state of severe shock and panic, I began yelling at them.

"THIS IS WHAT HAPPENS TO GOOD PEOPLE! THIS IS WHAT HAPPENS TO HONEST WOMEN! TO WIDOWS! I HATE THIS PLACE! I HATE ALL OF YOU! IT'S NOT FAIR… IT'S NOT FAIR… it's not… fair."

My voice trailed off as they sedated me with some kind of needle. I fell into a deep sleep and dreamed about Delores and her kids. They were all around a big Christmas tree, opening presents. Everyone was so happy as I watched them from the kitchen. This was my family and they brought me a great deal of joy.

Then I woke up in searing pain.

• • •

I spent a week in the hospital but it was three days before I apologized to the nurses whom I had verbally assaulted. The sensation in my back would go from dull to unimaginable pain all in the span of five seconds, and it would often knock me off my feet.

When I finally called Teresa to tell her what had happened, she panicked and insisted on coming over right away, which I thought was sweet. But I didn't want her to see me in such a weary state, so I said it wasn't all that bad. She persisted so I told her they weren't allowing any visitors. Her voice sounded hurt, which made me feel terrible. We said our goodbyes and I had a hard time pressing the END button on my phone. The truth is, I was in a bad place. I was mad at the world. My cynicism had finally birthed in me something very, very dark and I was even afraid to assess my current state of mind.

CHAPTER

10

I spent the next month working from home. The pain medications eventually became unnecessary and the scar healed up fairly well. What had not healed was my distrust of people and I sincerely questioned whether being kind to others was noble or naïve. Within a very short time span, I had attempted to help two individuals in need and both of those monumental efforts had netted zero results.

I couldn't get over the fact that Delores was dead. Like we all suspected, it was later confirmed that she had no traces of alcohol in her blood at the time of the accident. The poor girl had just fallen into a seizure and the officer who blew her tires out was only doing his job, trying to prevent the harm he ultimately caused. It's one of those situations that doesn't fall into black-and-white categories but resides somewhere in the gray area. It's those thoughts that torment my mind the most. What could've been done to prevent such a tragedy? Perhaps nothing.

Sleep had become difficult. Every time I began to drift off I'd see Delores and her kids exchanging gifts under that ugly, but earnest, Christmas tree. I wondered what would become of her children, but the thought was too depressing to entertain so I didn't even go there.

I mused over the stabbing and why it had occurred. To be honest, the answer to that never quite materialized. Why would a person so viciously turn on another who is only trying to help—someone who's putting his life on the line for a stranger! In the moment, and even afterward, the experience was so surreal that I could barely piece together the events of that night. And yet a month later, I couldn't get those same events out of my head.

I genuinely wanted to like people—I just couldn't do it anymore. The awful pain of rejection had been slowly cauterizing my heart over the years. It had become so calloused that only the simple things in life brought me any kind of pleasure, and none of them involved relationships with people. Human beings were unpredictable and complicated, something that I didn't need at the moment—or maybe ever.

Still, on days when I had the energy to dream I'd imagine myself giving the greatest speech in Oscar history and, through tears and a cracked voice, thanking my sweet wife, Teresa, who stood by my side through all the turmoil.

You have stirred my soul, I'd tell her.

Was it lame? Yes. But it's not like I stood in front of a mirror and acted out this whole scenario. No more than a couple times, anyway.

My father used to say, "A man with no spine is a jellyfish."

I presume the logic flowing from such a broken metaphor is that a lack of courage not only prompts softness of will, but can also sting others. It sometimes took me years to glean some sort of coherence from one of Pops' sayings but it was well worth the effort in most cases. My father read the Bible a lot and, over time, developed a real fondness for parables. The interesting thing about a parable is that the story hands out meaning on different levels: the surface level and the deep, or profound, level. Picking this up at a young age, I would always think very deeply about the words of my father, especially when they didn't seem to comport with whatever topic he was addressing at the time. For a while I thought Roger Graham was also speaking to me in parables but then I realized he was just genuinely stupid. There was nothing deep going on there.

My father studied philosophy in college and taught postgraduate studies at several universities before his death. He was fluent in French and Russian and could also read Koine Greek, which prompted a habit of always reading the New Testament in its original language. On Saturday afternoons he would line up parchments on a workbench in the garage and do his own translations, just to challenge himself.

After his death I was given a box containing several of those parchments, which are now safely kept in my bedroom closet. For obvious reasons, I could never bring myself to read them. I'm not a sappy person but that's sacred territory. When I came to Chicago from LA, one of the movers dropped my father's box into a puddle when taking it off the truck. I almost punched him in the face but then reasoned that assaulting a man over my father's Greek-to-English translation of Jesus' Sermon on the Mount was too ironic to warrant indulging.

All of these thoughts about Dad made me wonder whether or not he'd be happy with how I'd spent my life. My name had been in far-reaching magazines. I'd become a millionaire at a young age through nothing more than creativity and elbow grease. I was a powerful decision maker in a somewhat glorified industry and got to schmooze with the most famous people in the world. And yet, I was somehow convinced that Dad would not have been impressed with any of it. In fact, I could even picture him raising an eyebrow and saying, "Theo, are you honest? Have you been courageous? Are you a good person?"

The truth is that I had neither been honest nor courageous, at least not on all fronts. I harbored some kind of dysfunctional affection for Teresa but pretended I didn't. I put on a disguise around her and refused to be myself. Now that Roger's alien movie was in full swing, securing my current employment, and I had returned to good health, there was nothing more to lose. It was time.

CHAPTER

11

I sat in my office chair tapping a pen against the keyboard. A million things swam through my mind and I couldn't settle on any one thought. Maybe it was the two-and-a-half cups of coffee I'd drained by 9:30, or maybe I was just anxious to talk to her. And then, with a faint knock on the door, Teresa walked into my office.

She smiled, as she always did, and handed me the trades.

"Glad to see you back in action there, TL. Get it? Back in action… because your back is… okay, stupid joke. Too soon."

She was being extra-cute today, which made this hard. I hadn't really prepared anything. Perhaps this wasn't the right time. Okay, I needed to feel her out a little.

"You know, I've had a lot of time to think since the accident—reflecting on my life and everything."

She smiled and bobbed her head, waiting for me to say something useful but I couldn't find a good transition.

"Would you mind if I asked you a personal question?" I asked.

"You certainly may," she answered back, being chipper.

"If I had died that night, how many people do you think would have attended my funeral?"

Teresa looked at me as if the question made her uneasy. Uh oh, I was choking here.

"Wait, forget that—too morbid. What I'm saying is that, being so close to death makes you realize how lonely you really are—how each of us really needs each other. Do you know what I mean?"

"Yeah. I really do, Ted. I understand what you mean."

I was fishing for something more definitive.

"What do you see when you look at me, Teresa? No boss-employee stuff either. When you look at me as a man, just a guy off the street, what do you see?"

Her eyes lowered and she drew in a deep breath. She tightened her lips as though she was about to cry.

"Ted, a while back I said you should go out and meet some friends because you seem very unhappy to me. In the time I've worked for you, you've never seemed happy. I don't know what to say—it's hard to watch. You're so... guarded."

It was time. My heart was beating so fast that my speech began to tremble. I knew I had to say it at this moment or the words would never come.

"Teresa, I think I'm in love with you."

She put her hand to her mouth, mentally staggered. Guess she wasn't expecting that. My voice was feeble and nervous but I didn't care. The moment was here and she finally knew the truth.

"There it is. I'm in love with you and it's real. I know this may come as a surprise, but it's true. That's why I responded the way I did when you told me to meet some friends. You're the only friend I need. You're the only one I want to spend time with. I love the way you light up a room and the cute way that you talk. And I love… "

Teresa took a step back away from me.

"Ted, why are you doing this?"

"What do you mean? I'm telling you what I've been feeling for a while. Teresa, this is real."

"It's not."

"Yes, it is. I mean what I said."

"How could you do this to me?"

Her voice broke and she looked away. My heart began to crumble. She looked betrayed.

"Teresa, I don't want to make you feel awkward. But I know… if I don't tell you this, I can never forgive myself."

"Why are you doing this to me?" she repeated, her voice high and troubled.

"Just tell me you feel the same way."

Her eyes narrowed and I think she tried to force a laugh, but only a weak sound came out.

"You want me to tell you that I'm in love with you too? That's why you put me in this weird position?"

"I'm not trying to put you in a weird position," I apologized. "It's just… you're all I think about anymore."

"You're just lonely, Ted."

"No, I'm not… I mean, yes… but it's not *just* that! I've never obsessed over another person like this before."

"Obsessed?" she repeated, taken aback.

I knew I'd used the wrong word so I tried to recover by challenging her. "You've never felt like that about someone? I know you have."

"Ted, please…." she said, her voice begging. "Please just stop."

It began to dawn on me that I had made an epic mistake. The embarrassment was too much. I wanted to just run out of the room and hide in a cave. And yet, I had to stubbornly fight on.

"You don't have any feelings for me?" I probed further.

"Not like that," she said with a tender voice that was also shaking.

"Just have dinner with me tonight. You might not feel anything right now, but give it a chance. Please."

"Ted, I can't do that," she said while staring at the floor. "I just can't."

"So, what… you're busy then?"

"No," she said. "I'm so sorry but I just don't feel that way about you."

I honestly had not expected this level of rejection. I began to feel sick.

"Is this because we work together?"

She looked at me so sweetly and said, "It's not."

"So there's no chance that we will ever be... I mean, there's no spark at all for you?"

A tear rolled down her cheek and that cemented the issue with me. This dream was vapor.

She sniffled and said, "You're a good man, but this isn't for us. I'm so sorry, Ted. This isn't for us."

I had no idea what to do next.

"Um, could you grab me the expenditures from last week?" I said for no reason whatsoever.

Teresa nodded, wiped her eyes, and walked out.

She gave her resignation a week later.

CHAPTER

12

I was still in a fog the day Teresa left. I took a detour on the way home just to get my mind right. I was angry that she didn't love me back, even just a little bit. "What is so terrible about me?" I began to wonder. A-list actresses knew me by name and yet plain-Jane Teresa somehow thought it revolting to imagine a relationship with me. I had a name in the industry and made millions, but it wasn't enough for Teresa. How ridiculous to consider being with a man who would actually care about her and sacrifice everything to be with her. I pictured her ending up with some guy with a tribal tattoo who stays out until 2 o'clock in the morning while she anxiously waits for him at home, wondering how many girls he'd hooked up with at the club. Part of me wanted her to end up with a guy like that just so she'd feel terrible about rejecting the nice guy. I wanted to drown my anger in alcohol as the rage set in. Self-pity began coursing through my veins like heroin and I felt like running my car into Lake Michigan. "Would anyone even care?" I asked aloud, almost shouting at myself.

At the point where I actually began to consider ending it all, Delores entered my mind again almost as if by divine revelation. Immediately, I changed course and drove to Delores' old neighborhood. The memory of us in her living room with the kids, all happy and without a care in the world, was vividly clear. That had been the first time in a long time that I'd felt a sense of kinship with other people. And now that my hopes for a relationship with Teresa had been dashed, to put it mildly, I wondered if something else was destined for me. Maybe even a life without relationships. Jean-Paul Sartre once said, "Hell is other people." I was inclined to agree at this point in my life.

• • •

That night I ate pizza at a sports bar with Greg, the line producer on the alien film Roger had set in motion. As he dredged on about market analysis and release dates, my eyes were drawn to the big television set above the bar. A news reporter, standing in front of crime scene tape, spoke to the camera about an elderly couple that had been shot down in front of their home. As she was speaking a little scroll began at the bottom of the screen announcing some breaking news about a politician who had just committed suicide. I heard a finger being snapped and realized that Greg had asked me a question. I had completely zoned out.

"I'm sorry—what were you saying?"

"We need to push the release date up two weeks so we're not competing with the Spielberg flick."

"That's fine," I said, not caring an ounce.

I left the pizza joint feeling very uneasy and it had nothing to do with the food, which I usually enjoy. But tonight even our Chicago deep dish tasted flat. In fact, nothing seemed quite right in the world. Traffic was unusually busy and I was tired of sitting in my car all the time. I flipped on the radio to ease the ride home but the news station had nothing positive to say about anything in the world. I slipped in a CD, a compilation of my favorite classics, but even that sounded off.

Was I losing it? Was my mind so fragile that I couldn't even stomach my favorite things any longer? These thoughts swam around the entire ride home and even invaded my bedroom. I tossed and turned all night, unable to sleep.

Around 4 am I clumsily stepped into my home office and sat down at the computer. Unable to retain a single thought for more than a few seconds, I began to search the web—for hours. I was looking for an escape, the real thing. And that required research.

CHAPTER

13

After three weeks of research, I knew exactly two things: I was going to buy an island, and I was going to live alone. The idea didn't scare me nearly as much as it should have. I was simply tired of it all. I was tired of pressure and stress, I was tired of watching good women go for the wrong guys, I was tired of violence and death I was tired of feeling like I didn't belong in the world that presently existed. Fortunately for me, I could actually do something about it.

Over the next few weeks I met with an international real estate broker, a green technology expert, three professional survivalists and numerous other contractors and specialists. Things were taking shape, and this weird fantasy I'd spun for myself was looking more and more like reality.

Roger hadn't given me a lot to do on the new movie so I basically sleepwalked through pre-production, doing only the bare minimum while tending to my extensive planning. However, as the day of my departure drew near, I knew I'd have to actually talk to Roger about my plans. It's not that I needed his blessing, but, despite his many issues, he was the one who had given me a job in the first place, a job which ultimately made this decision even possible. So I checked the calendar on my phone and saw only two remaining appointments before leaving this life behind for good. The first appointment was with Roger. The second, a speech at NYU.

• • •

I headed into Roger's office, that sweet aroma of cigar smoke hitting me in the face the moment I stepped inside. He was on a phone call so he gave me the "one sec" finger gesture. After howling with laughter, he slapped his knee, said goodbye and hung up the phone.

He then turned to me and said, "What's up, Teddy? Did Greg tell you we decided to move the release date again?"

"I'm quitting, Roger."

He looked at me like I'd just punched his mother.

"Say what now?" He responded.

"I'm done. I'm out. This is—I can't work here anymore. I'm done with movies."

"Teddy, if you needed a raise you could've just asked. You want me to talk to Jerry?"

"This isn't about my salary, Roger. I'm leaving town."

"That's not a bad idea—you deserve some time off. Why don't we talk about this whole thing when you get back from your vacation."

"Not a vacation," I said as I slid a folded, stapled report out of my breast pocket and handed it to him.

He looked at the image on the front, which I'd printed off of the internet, and then his eyes drifted back up to me.

"I bought it."

"An island? You're buying an island?"

"It's all taken care of. I bought a house, five thousand square feet on three miles of beach. No other residents, just me, the waves and satellite TV. No distractions, no worries. Food comes in by boat twice a month. I designed everything—it's perfect."

"What about electricity?" he asked, just to humor me. Roger probably saw this as an early midlife crisis or some kind of nervous breakdown.

"It's all solar. Cost me a little extra but I'll have my own self-sufficient energy. It's truly paradise. I've left no stone unturned with this thing."

"It's isolationism, Ted. I know you've had some relationship problems but come on now, this is nuts."

"I've been planning this for months. I just didn't have the nerve to pull the trigger until recently. I called my real estate guy in the Philippines this morning. Everything is final."

"That's in Asia. Are you putting me on here?" He said in shock. "Get a summer home in the Keys for crying out loud. Come on, Ted."

"The money has already changed hands. There's no turning back now."

Roger took an unusually long pause, snuffed out his cigar, and crossed over to me. I saw him searching for the words to say but somehow he knew I was serious. He then did something much unexpected—he reached over and gave me a tight hug. This wasn't a "see ya, loser" kind of hug; it was a genuine, almost fatherly gesture that I'd never witnessed from the man. I was a bit taken aback. As we broke apart he looked remorseful.

"You'll be back in a month," he said, believing it with all his heart.

• • •

They had postponed my lecture at NYU because of the stabbing but tonight I would give my talk. The topic was on *the essence of being a producer*, but I had decided on the ride over that, being my last appointment ever I should change the subject and talk about something closer to my heart. After all, the life of a producer is not one that anyone should envy and I was tired of pretense. I wanted to speak my mind and offer a farewell speech of sorts.

It was the first time I wasn't nervous for an event and even Jerry showed up backstage to see how I was doing. He hadn't heard the news, which made me feel slightly bad for him.

"You go on in five. How do you feel?"

"Jerry, you might want to leave early for this one."

He looked at me, puzzled.

"Trust me—this is my last talk."

"Okay, okay… it's not an issue."

I was sad as I looked at Jerry. He wasn't much of a friend but he was all I had.

"I'm going to miss you, old boy," I said.

He was perplexed as the stagehand came and grabbed me, ushering me to the curtain.

I took the podium and cleared my throat. What most people don't know is that giving a speech in an auditorium is a strange experience. The stage lights prevent you from seeing your audience, so it's like looking out into a sea of black. And that made what I had to say a lot easier.

"I was asked to come here and give a talk on the essence of being a producer. But on the way over, I thought about sharing something a little different with you all. Something you can take with you. Something from my heart."

I could hear a quiet murmur in the audience but still couldn't see them. Jerry told me it was a packed house.

"I lost my mother at nine and my father at nineteen. It occurred to me recently that I'm probably the only person on the planet who still remembers their names. Just me.

I'm an only child without a single confidant in my life. But my companions are varied. They include Vivaldi, red wine and TV news. This is what gets me by. I've known tragedy and I've certainly known heartache. I also know what it's like to live the American Dream. I drive a Lexus LS 600 and my bills are always paid. I don't worry about healthcare expenses. And yet my encounters have not left me with a positive view of mankind.

Don't chase what I have; it's hollow, at best. Appreciate this moment in time because you may not have another. I guess the truth, when you get right down to it, is that we are all alone in life. All of us. Community is a myth. Solidarity is gone. Someone might as well say it. So stay true to yourself because it's all you've got.

You'll forgive me for ending this so abruptly but what I really wanted to say to you all... to humanity, is—goodbye. It was a good ride while it lasted but I just don't need you anymore."

I heard some murmurs out in the audience.

"Thank you for this evening. I'm sure the other speakers will do a better job of entertaining you guys, but I have a plane to catch."

CHAPTER

14

Sitting in the airport, the trip seemed daunting but the anticipation of a new adventure left swarms of butterflies in my belly. I was positively giddy. Ahead of me lay a seventeen-hour flight to Manila, another local flight to Cebu City, an eight-hour jeep ride to a ferryboat, which, a day later, would put me at the docks of Surigao, near the location where my land was nestled.

I picked an island close to the mainland just in case I got stir-crazy and also for medical attention if such were ever needed.

Working in the film business for more than a decade left me with very identifiable mental defects, one of which was the inability to not look at real-life situations and ponder whether they would make a good movie. Every event became a plot point in a screenplay and people were characters written on white paper. Some were fascinating and some needed a re-write.

One such person had just sat down next to me, fighting to control a half-dozen screaming kids. I kept reading the Voltaire paperback in my hands but still felt her looking at me. I never understood how it is one could feel another person looking at him but my radar was definitely picking up signals. A quick glance up proved that I was right. She smiled politely.

"You are going to Philippines, no?"

"I am. Yes."

"I'm going Manila. You?"

"Cebu. Then Surigao. It's complicated."

She nodded.

"Ah, that place is very nice. You like there. I was in Cebu three years ago. They have a different dialect than my place. You speak Tagalog? That's our national language."

Conceding the obvious, I nodded "no."

"Oh, you must learn. Very important. You are white so they will take advantage of you there."

"I don't think that'll be a problem in the place I'm going," I said with a smile.

She wasn't even listening.

"We learn English from grade school. It's required in our place. They teach university using English."

"Interesting."

"We Filipinos are very fond of Americans since MacArthur liberate us from Japanese during the war."

Would this lady ever stop talking?

"You not married?" she asked.

"No."

"You have a special person there in Philippines?"

"I do not."

"Maybe you find a beautiful lover there."

"Doubtful. But thank you."

She looked at me strangely, probably hoping her seat on the plane wasn't next to mine.

"It's not good to be alone," she said, before shouting at her children in a strange dialect.

"Well, I hope all Filipinos are as welcoming as you," I lied.

They had called for first class passengers to board five minutes ago, but I had been distracted by this woman and her gang of miniature hoodlums.

• • •

Stepping onto the ramp and through the door hatch of the plane, I began to feel nostalgic. Our layover was in Japan so this would likely be the last time my feet would stand on American soil. The thought gave me pause and I stood in the door long enough to catch an impatient jolt from a gentleman behind me as his carry-on luggage hit me between the shoulders.

"Sorry," he quipped, not meaning it.

I moved aside and let him filter through coach as I turned left and ducked into first class. I shoved my backpack into the overhead bin and sat down.

How long would I mourn America, the land of my birth and the only culture I knew? Was I having second thoughts? There was still time to run, I thought to myself. People were still filing onto the plane. Sure, it would be embarrassing but this was my only chance.

Turn around! Do it!

Sudden fear gripped me like a vise. My throat was already dry and I began to sweat. A strange thing happens when your adrenaline is racing: little things around you suddenly take on profound meaning and you wonder why you've never paid attention to them before. A young flight attendant had leaned over to close the bins in front of me and I noticed her wedding ring. This woman who risks her life to make me comfortable on a flying machine is someone's wife. Someone loves this woman and prays for her safe return every day. My heart beat even faster. She noticed my panic.

"Are you okay, sir? Would you like a magazine?"

A magazine? Lady, get off this plane and race home to your husband. He loves you!

"Sir?" She said, concerned.

"Water. I could use some water."

She smiled and pointed to the complimentary bottle of water stuck to the side of my armrest.

"Of course. Thank you."

I took a giant swig from the bottle, almost finishing the whole thing in a single gulp. Then I heard the plane's door being latched.

"No!" I thought to myself. "It's too late and I haven't even made my decision yet. This flight attendant lady distracted me!"

The captain's screechy voice came on.

"Welcome aboard. We have a non-stop to Tokyo, Japan. Expect some bumpy skies in the first hour or so. Arrival time in Japan should be around nine o'clock in the evening, which is about thirteen hours from now. For those of you continuing on to the Philippines, it'll be an additional four hours to Manila. Enjoy your flight."

An electronic pop from the intercom and that was that. It had become official. I was leaving the United States of America to live on an island off the coast of the Philippines.

Holy crap! was the thought running through my head. *I'm actually doing this!*

My internal monologue was so loud that I wondered if others beside me could hear it. We began to taxi the runway and I felt nauseous. Could it be that a fantasy spawned in a fifth grade nurse's lounge might actually come to fruition? I was going to find out.

CHAPTER

15

Two hours into the flight, my mind began to settle. Yet the familiar mechanical hiss of the plane never quite allowed me to be at ease. I looked down and found that my fists were clenched. It's a rare occasion when I can actually sleep during any mode of travel and this was no exception. I shared the front of the plane with a businessman who had been punching something into his iPad since we took off, as well as an Asian guy in wire-rimmed glasses. Neither of them looked like they wanted to be here. I relaxed my head on the pillow, reclining a bit, to see if sleep would elude me once more. It did not.

I dreamed of Delores and her kids again. When I woke up a couple of hours later, it took about thirty seconds to get my bearings and understand that I was on a plane heading somewhere. Looking up at my personal, flat-panel TV, I saw a crude computer graphic of a plane cresting the Canadian coast. My back was sore and many more hours lay ahead. When you hate to travel as much as I do, visualizing the destination can help to get you through. I had seen blueprints of the house and tiny web photos of the island itself but I couldn't help but imagine what it would feel like to actually stand there and gaze upon it. That thought managed to soothe my achy legs for the duration of the flight to Japan.

It was dark when we landed at Tokyo-Narita and boy was I relieved to stretch my legs! Inside the terminal I stumbled two very weak legs into the restroom across from a Hello Kitty gift shop, where I found the urinals full. Undeterred, I stepped into a stall to find a plastic toilet seat… on the floor. It looked clean, but foreign. That's when it first hit me and Toto that we weren't in Kansas anymore. The bizarre Japanese directions, and equally bizarre stick-men cartoons, didn't help matters. After a quick squirt, I went back to await the one-hour layover. Despite being delirious from travel, I kept a positive attitude and enjoyed a seaweed and chocolate flavored Kit-Kat from the gift shop.

In just a short time, I'd be in my new country of residence with a world of possibilities ahead.

The smooth, four-hour flight felt like twenty minutes. As the pilot hovered for our final approach, I saw the Manila Bay glistening with lights from buildings and streets at two o'clock in the morning. All the activity below reminded me of flying over New York City. Things seemed so peaceful from this altitude. Don't Filipinos ever sleep? The descent seemed to take forever but we finally touched down at Ninoy Aquino airport at 2:18 am. I was home.

CHAPTER

16

I stepped out of the plane's hatch and headed down a beige corridor leading to the terminal. The place smelled fragrant and sweet, which surprised me. I began noticing the posters and cardboard advertisements in the airport hallways—they were for products I'd never heard of and the models didn't look like anyone I knew. I was also the only white person in sight.

At the end of the hallway I came to a large, open room full of crowded travelers. I could see the luggage carousels but they were behind metal bars and a turnstile. I'd been told we had to go through a checkpoint before we could get our bags but I had all my personal items shipped to the island in advance, with the exception of a carry-on backpack.

Turns out, it didn't matter. A very pretty woman at the front desk told me I had to go through the line with my passport to get it stamped. After two hours of standing in an absurdly long line, I got my first passport stamp and headed through the gates, where an equally long line of taxis was waiting to take folks to the domestic airport. A young boy spotted me immediately and ran over.

"Backpack. I'll carry. I'll carry."

Not having been born yesterday, I realized this kid was trying to earn a little cash. Since I hardly needed his assistance, I simply gave him two one-dollar bills from my pocket, the remnants of a trip to Starbucks back in Chicago. *How strange that seemed at this moment.*

The kid smiled widely and ran back to his post. I nodded to the first cab driver that I saw. Without asking a question, or bothering to smile, he took my backpack and put it in the back of his cab. Then he stood there, perhaps waiting for me to speak. I knew from my research that nearly all Filipinos speak English, so I dove right in.

"I need a hotel close to here. I'm leaving tomorrow morning, early."

"You want City Garden. Is cheap," he said.

Maybe he mistook "cheap" for "close" but I hardly felt like arguing. The guy was nice and had work to do.

So far things seemed a bit foreign, for obvious reasons, but nothing too out of the ordinary—and then we pulled out of the airport carousel and into the street, where I got my first glimpse of the city. Yep, it was actually *very* out of the ordinary.

The first thing that assaulted my senses was the scent. My driver had his window cracked, which resulted in my getting blasted with this strange aroma which felt almost tangible. To best describe it, I'd say it's a mixture of gasoline and barbecue smoke. It was intoxicating and made my head spin as we whipped through narrow urban streets.

Bundles of tangled telephone cable hung like drapes over the sidewalk, stretching as far as the eye could see. All the roadside buildings were made from concrete and the sidewalks were busted and littered with garbage.

My eyes were trying to catch up. Everything I saw flying past my window was something I'd never seen before, so it was hard trying to comprehend everything. Herds of motorcycles and Pedicabs jockeyed for position on the cracked concrete street, each weaving in and out of a wide cluster of traffic. Despite being very late at night—or very early in the morning, depending on one's perspective—there were people literally everywhere. Guys selling food from carts on the sidewalk; teenage girls walking in packs with their friends; and drunk people spilling out of bars and clubs. A night out in Chicago or LA had nothing on this place; it was excessively crowded, and noisy.

The next assault took place on my equilibrium, thanks to the cab driver. I would later come to discover that everyone in the Philippines, cabbie or not, drives like he is in the Indianapolis 500. It's bizarre and frightening, yet I somehow felt safe inside that taxi. What shocked my western brain the most was the local custom of cars literally nudging one another out of the way—I mean, physically nudging other cars to merge. There are no lanes, just a strange game of chicken in which the right of way goes to the one who is least afraid to die.

After twenty minutes of sensory overload, we arrived at City Garden Hotel and I remembered that I hadn't exchanged any Filipino currency yet.

"Sir, excuse me, but I only have dollar bills."

He looked in the rearview.

"I can take Filipino pesos only. Sorry."

I was confused and desperate.

"Is there an ATM where I can exchange?"

"Ano yan? ATM. What that is?"

"Like a—place to exchange?"

He nodded.

"Hotel should exchange for you. Just pay your room. I'll turn off meter."

This ordeal took up thirty minutes of my time but the fare was paid and I retired for the evening.

The hotel room was small but ornate. There was an air conditioner unit in the window and the room smelled of old, dusty blankets. But when I sat down on the bed I felt the world fall away. It's hard to describe the release I felt at that moment, but it was glorious. I laid back on the bed and flipped on the TV to see the evening news. A man on a motorcycle had apparently been hit by a bus. Unlike the evening news back in the States, they actually show dead bodies on TV over here. And not the blurred-out kind.

After a striking image of two legs under a bus and what appeared to be a head resting next to the front tire, I decided to flip over to MTV Asia where scantily clad Korean girls danced along with a rap tune. I changed the channel once more to see several commercials in a row for products and brands I never knew existed. Enough of that—I switched the TV off and closed my eyes.

I slept straight through for five hours until the alarm on my phone went off. Fumbling around on the side table, I managed to knock a lamp over before silencing the phone. I woke up in a daze, not sure where I was. After a few seconds it sunk in. Here I was, locked in this alternate universe again. My senses couldn't catch up.

Nearing the window, which overlooks a busy street, I witnessed car horns ablaze during morning rush hour. It was chaos in a haze of fog.

"How did I sleep through this noise?" I wondered aloud.

I needed to make final preparations for the last leg of travel, so I picked up the phone and dialed an agency I had been working with.

"This is Ted LaSalle again. I'm staying at City Garden in Makati. Can you send a driver?"

The response was quick. After thirty minutes, I was off to the domestic airport where I boarded a Cebu Pacific A380 and sat back for a one-hour flight. The landing was rougher than I cared for, but at least we were on the ground. It occurred to me that this would probably be my last flight anywhere, so that relaxed me a bit. Planes would be a thing of the past for Ted LaSalle.

The sun scorched my bare arms and legs as I left the hatch and stepped out onto the mobile stair unit they'd wheeled over. The heat left me breathless for a moment, the glowing sky burning a whole into my forehead. I prayed the rest of the journey would be air conditioned. Otherwise, heat stroke would became a real possibility.

CHAPTER

17

The executive travel agency had sent over a dusty, white van with bald tires. I exchanged pleasantries with the driver, who spoke only broken English, and settled in for a bumpy, six-hour ride. Very little was said during the commute so I just stared out the window and tried not to think about my aching back muscles and sweat-drenched t-shirt.

The scenery exhausted my eyes. It was like biting into some food you're not familiar with: the moment it hits your tongue, your mind revolts. That's the feeling. The Philippines, from the city to the countryside, is both breathtakingly beautiful and horrendously ugly at the same time, depending on which direction your head is facing. The rice fields under a glistening sun were a pleasant sight that made me feel serene and removed from the current era. But across the street were row after row of tin shed, muddy, bamboo housing along with countless Tanduay billboards, which is some kind of Filipino rum. The driver offered me something to drink and I accepted with only slight hesitation. He pulled onto the shoulder and talked to some guys standing in front of a storefront shack for about ten minutes before going inside. He came out with a glass bottle of Coke and handed it to me. It was only half cold but it would do.

That familiar aroma was always around, that scent of faint gasoline mixed with barbecue smoke. The countryside, or province, of the Philippines looked a lot different than remote areas in the States. Back home, the country is where you go to seclude yourself and get away from people. Over here, the dirt and gravel roads are almost as populated as the urban centers.

Smoke plumed from shanty houses stretching as far as the eye could see. Though I was just in transit to a much different part of the country, it occurred to me that I could be happy in a place like this; not entirely comfortable, but happy. Little Filipino kids waved at me as we drove past. Things were uncomplicated here.

We arrived at the docks late in the afternoon. It was still insanely hot. I handed my ticket to a physically imposing Australian man with a surfer's cut.

"They call you Joe?" he asked.

"No, I'm Ted."

"I mean the locals. They call you Joe?"

"Not that I'm aware."

He grinned at that.

"They call all white people 'Joe' over here. Australian, German—whatever. We're all American to them."

I gave a weary, but intrigued, dip of the head.

"The people have been pretty nice," I commented.

"That's because you're kano," he told me while checking my ticket.

"What's a kano?" I asked of the word that sounded like "kah-no."

He smiled.

"White. Kano means you're white. They like that. Mosquitoes too—they love white meat over here."

Just then, a herd of Filipino soldiers in military fatigues stormed past, scaring me half to death. The Australian man noticed the alarm on my face.

"Don't worry about that, mate... just Abu Sayyaf stirring up some dust down in Mindanao. That's a long way from where you're headed."

"Where I'm going is a long way from anything," I corrected.

"No worries, ay?" he said.

"No worries."

The ferry boat was reminiscent of small cruise ships in the US but without the amenities. I sat on the stern as we toiled along through deep blue waters. The setting sun was a brilliant orange whose glow was being mirrored by the ocean below. Sharing the deck with me were several Filipino couples who stood against the railing.

The sun felt warm against my skin as gently pushing wind cooled it. The dipping and bobbing of the vessel against the sea became hypnotic.

"This is why I came," I thought to myself.

As the hours passed, it became evident that whatever fate I was heading toward could not be reversed. There was a time, back in the hotel room in Manila, when I thought it might still be possible to change plans and head back to the States. After all, the airport was only a twenty-minute ride away and even despite the grueling flights, it was still possible to return. But now, so far away from that hotel room in Manila, it truly sunk in: I couldn't turn around now. I was in far too deep.

I slept for a couple of hours in a compartment of humble means until my bladder woke me up. I popped into the hallway and flagged down a Filipino attendant.

"Yes, sir?" she asked.

"How long until we dock in Surigao?"

She took a moment to count in her head.

"Nineteen hours more," she said brightly.

Wow, my guesstimate was way off. I figured a couple of hours, tops.

"Can you point me to the bathroom?"

"The CR is right behind that door," she said, pointing to the end of the hall.

"CR?" I said, not sure she understood.

"Comfort Room. You must go, yeah?"

I nodded, slightly embarrassed, and headed down the hallway where I found a door marked:

Under repairing!

Stepping inside the restroom, I immediately jumped in horror. My eyes drifted to a wooden bowl and a plastic bucket filled halfway to the top with murky water. I latched the tiny door with a metal pin and searched for toilet paper, as my bladder had sent a false alarm. My lunch was either coming up or going down—hopefully the latter.

Behind the bucket, my hand found a cardboard roll with two squares of tissue left intact. I removed the tissue from the cardboard with surgical precision. The moment I dropped trou, the boat swayed violently to my left. I lost balance and fell down onto my side, pants around my ankles. The boat then corrected itself but not before the bowl of excrement spilled onto my back, at which point I let a few expletives fly. I heard a couple of Filipino girls giggling out in the hallway.

"Ay naku!" I heard, muffled by the door.

That's the Filipino version of "Good lord!" apparently. I cleaned myself off with the dirty water from the bucket, finished my business and went back to my cabin for the remainder of the trip.

• • •

As we docked on the northern tip of Surigao City, loads of people began to exit the ferry boat—none of whom were

American, save one. As the lone "Joe," I moved past swarms of travelers, incredulous of the various displays of affection. I didn't come all this way to watch people hug one another. And yes, by this point in the trip, I had become a little irritable.

I was supposed to meet a guy named Nako who owned a boat. He was described to me as a friendly Japanese man about my height, which is a rare thing over here. Not seeing anyone fitting that description, I approached an elderly Filipino woman who looked like she was waiting on someone.

"Hi, I'm looking for South Pacific Endeavors."

She just looked at me.

"It's a small charter boat."

I received another blank stare. I then heard a voice behind me:

"She speak Surigaonon, no English."

I turned and saw a smiling Japanese man wearing a baseball cap. He offered his hand.

"South Pacific Endeavors, I'm Nako."

"I'm Ted. We spoke on the phone."

"Everything is ready. Your real estate guy was here this morning. He make sure everything as you request."

"Thank you, Nako. Shall we?"

Nako led me to a small, but clean, vessel roped off on the other side of the docks. If I had to guess, I'd say from the furnishings that he lived on the boat.

"Your personal item all arrive on island already. They beat you here," he said with a hearty laugh.

My energy was spent.

"So how long is the trip?" I asked, expecting the worst.

"Forty-five minute," he said. "You close."

The words, "Thank God," fell out of my mouth.

• • •

My lengthy trip from Chicago to this place had given me more resolve than ever that this is what I wanted. People were trouble. People complicated things. People were only needed in small doses. When I told a guy on the ferry that I moved here to get away from the evils of humanity, he asked if I was intending to live a celibate life. Indeed, that is the cost of moving to your own island. However, there were provisions made for this. If I ever got to the point where I could no longer stand the sexual tension, it was only a short trip to the mainland where, in desperate times, I could cast a wide net and hope for some kind of companionship. Finding someone to party with could be done, with only slight inconvenience.

I'm not talking about prostitution, mind you. My desperation would never sink to paying for sex. But, as in the US, casual relationships are not uncommon in these parts. I'd never been prone to such behavior but my world was looking more and more foreign these days.

The life I'd left behind would serve as the subject of reflection to sweep away boredom but would not be any indication of future behavior. Truly I had started over. Nobody knew me over here, so as long as I could get along with myself—something I've managed for well over thirty years—then all would be well.

• • •

Nako steered the boat through peaceful waters. I found myself below deck, vomiting into a rice bag. Everyone says, "Don't drink the water," but when you're thirsty and there's not a bottle of Aquafina in sight, you do what you have to do. And I paid for it. I rinsed my mouth with soda, spitting into the little sink. Nako saw me through the hatch and just shook his head.

Americans.

"You feel better in five minute," he said. "Almost home, my friend."

What a beautiful thing to hear. It completely made up for the terrible trip. I joined Nako above deck and sat next to him on top of a heavy box.

"Can't wait," I said.

"One thing first," Nako said with a grin. "Your agent, Mr. Yano, he say this island not inhabited."

"Right. It's just me."

"But your place is offshore from Surigao. That mean it appears on map as unclaim."

"Okay?" I said, not sure where this was going.

"You must name island for geographers. Government need to tax on paperwork."

I took a moment.

"The Island of Ted. That work?"

"Work for me," Nako said. "I don't live there."

CHAPTER

18

As Nako and I finished our laugh on the bow of this little charter boat, my eyes looked up and beheld it—the island. We were still a bit shy of docking but the water had already caught my attention. It was translucent blue and even this far from shore, I could see the bottom floor of the ocean. I felt like jumping out to swim the rest of the way but wanted to restrain my childlike wonder for fear of embarrassing myself, or Americans in general, in front of Nako.

It was paradise, true and utter beauty in every direction. Waves lapped against the sides of the boat as we trolled to a rest against a small wooden dock leading to white sand. A thick row of palm trees sat twenty yards aground and skirted around like a curtain. I immediately leaped off the boat and sunk my toes in the sandy beach.

I looked back as Nako tied off the boat.

"Nako, this place is a post card!"

"Yeah, it's okay. Listen, I bring you food last evening. Two week supply as you request."

Although I had only seen a tiny beach and a wall of palm trees, all regrets began to fade away. I felt a sense of pride.

This was my island. My sand. My palm trees. And for a quarter-mile out to sea, my ocean too!

"I can't believe this place," I said in wonder.

"Wait until you see the house," Nako teased.

After securing the boat, we took a sandy, but well-carved, dirt path through the palm tree forest. A lizard ran across my foot and shot toward the water. A new pet, maybe?

Nako and I walked uphill for around ten minutes before we came to a clearing. There we started a slight descent for a few paces and the wall of palm trees broke open to reveal a house in the distance, sitting at the base of a large hill with terraces lining the sides. It was my new home.

The house was an exquisitely designed piece of architecture with Tuscan and Spanish flare, including a courtyard at the center. It was accented with glass and bamboo with massive stone walls. It shouted of palatial grandeur, with the exception of a rather out-of-place looking satellite dish mounted on the far edge of the roof. The house was a massive oasis of tranquility. A sculpted patch of lawn lay around the perimeter, with stone and brick carving out a nice circular walkway up to the porch.

No cars on this island but it was a nice thought.

"That your solar panels on left side of property," Nako pointed out. "On the right you see lagoon and in the rear is rice field. These hills are terraced but no one cultivate yet.

Roof is reinforced with special oak for rainy season. You'll need that."

We stopped at the entrance and I dropped my bags, mouth agape.

Nako said, "You also have coconut tree all around house. In forest you have palm and banana but mostly bamboo. This good for building project."

Nako then handed me a set of keys and a card that read: "Thank you for doing business, valued customer!"

"It was my pleasure serve you, Mr. LaSalle. Welcome to Island of Ted. I see you in two week. Call me you need anything."

"Thank you, Nako."

We shook hands and Nako made his way back to the dirt path. I watched him go with a wave and felt a cool breeze passing across my face. The palm trees in the distance swayed as the gentle wind blew, ruffling the wide leaves. That sound—those leaves dancing in the breeze—gave me a feeling in my gut that I had longed for since childhood. I closed my eyes and just breathed... and listened. Heaven.

• • •

Stepping into my giant enclave, I first noticed how quiet it was. I should have expected that, granted, but the lack of sound made everything feel so sterile. It was obvious that I was standing in a new construction, a fact evidenced by the strong smell of paint and newly polished wood trim. For a moment the whole enterprise seemed eerie. I walked through an enormous kitchen and thought of all the great meals I'd cook and enjoy on the peaceful bamboo deck, far away from the ills besetting the other side of the world. Here there was no violence, no oppression, no evil, no… people.

Moving up the stairs I caught a glimpse of the ground floor of the house. The first thought that occurred to me, and one I'd need to forget, was how nice it would be to show this to someone else. After consciously deleting that thought, I continued on into the master bedroom. It was breathtaking: twenty-by-thirty feet with a giant bed and exquisite Neo-Asian décor.

At the far end of the room, huge doors of fogged glass opened to reveal a second-story view of the back yard—and some back yard it was! Beyond a small, man-made lagoon was thick, lush forest. I always had an affinity for palm trees and now I owned a couple thousand of them. I wasn't sure how far the forest stretched or what the beach on the opposite end of the island looked like. Such curiosity was meant for a less tiresome day, one in which walking for hours seemed ideal.

There was much more of the house to see but for some inexplicable reason, I simply sat down on the bed and took a nap. Within seconds I had fallen into deep sleep and for the first time in months, I didn't dream about Delores or the kids. I dreamed of a woman, perhaps my Filipino nurse at the hospital, massaging my scalp with different oils. Being touched in such a delicate way soothed me, and that feeling stayed with me even after waking up to see that it was dark outside. I checked my watch and saw that I had slept for six hours. Wow.

Checking out the rest of the house, I decided to explore my designer toilet. It lived up to the hype. Next was the shower, and boy did I need a shower. My first thought, while undressing, was to close the doors leading out to my deck. It would take some time for the thought to really sink in: You are alone here. Like… really, really, really alone. No need to draw the blinds—ever.

That night I cracked open the fridge and saw that Nako had pre-stocked several items and had even left a dinner tray full of some kind of homemade noodle dish in the center. It was a nice gesture, but I pushed it aside and grabbed a plate of Filipino egg rolls, called lumpia, which had been ordered from a local resort café ahead of time. I mowed through them with a glass of chilled merlot and sat down in front of a 100-inch TV. After fumbling with the controls, I managed to figure out how to turn the system on and engage the satellite dish. It was so quiet that I could actually hear the satellite dish turning outside.

"How bizarre," I thought.

Since I'd slept through the afternoon, I was now wide awake at midnight. This time difference thing would eventually work itself out as I became acclimated to being twelve hours in the future. Chicago was but a dim memory now and it felt wonderful.

CHAPTER

19

Two weeks after my arrival, I was still learning about the house. There were little cabinets hidden everywhere and I discovered that all of the bedroom windows could change shades, from fogged to clear, by hitting a little dial on the wall. The button was initially hidden by a large plant so you'll excuse the lack of awareness.

Every morning I woke up around seven and enjoyed fresh coffee out on the veranda, which was partially covered by a bamboo ceiling—helpful during a surprise rain shower. I'd watch the sunrise sparkle off my fake lagoon, a.k.a. the mossy pool, and when it became especially hot in the afternoons I would jump in for a quick swim. The days passed surprisingly quickly and I had to force myself not to spend too much time watching TV or surfing the internet. Every so often, I'd check out BBC News just to see all of the nonsense from which I had been rescued. The world had gone on without me as well: Al Qaeda was still suicide bombing the crap out of third-world shitholes and the stock market was down again. There were a slew of celebrity break-ups and another politician got caught with his pants down.

Good riddance.

In an effort to keep things completely honest, my paradise was not without its downside. For me, it was loneliness. After a particularly funny re-run of Jimmy Fallon, I let out a strained, almost silent laugh from my belly. I had nearly lost my voice from not talking to anyone in two weeks. My dreams were often filled with the sensation of being touched or caressed by other people. These dreams weren't sexual at all, just echoes of companionship.

Another decidedly more embarrassing downside was what I call "scared child syndrome." I lived on a rather large island, filled with trees that made noises when the wind blew and critters that dashed around in the shadows. Things definitely go bump in the night. I'm a rational man who knows that there's no one else around for miles, and separated by deep ocean at that. I also knew that ghosts and spirits don't exist. Nevertheless, on a still night I'd find my heart racing after hearing an unexpected noise outside my door. For that reason, I often kept the stereo playing soft, classical music after I retired the TV each night. It fills in the silence quite well but it's not loud enough to prevent quality sleep.

On my fourteenth night on the island I was watching a CSI re-run when something caught my eye out the living room window. I could have sworn there was a reflection coming from the front of the property. I silenced the TV and stood up, wearing tennis shoes and a bathrobe. The place fell silent. My ears became more and more attuned to the natural noises around me.

"Are those footsteps?" I asked myself silently.

Not particularly giving a flip, I swung the front door open and stood on the concrete porch as boldly as I could pretend.

Who am I, Clint Eastwood? Then I saw something in the forest.

My adrenaline surged. This time I knew something was there. For some reason I can't explain, I ran toward it. It moved away from me at lightning speed!

Trees and twigs snapped past as I cut through the warm night air at full speed. I once heard that if a lion charges you in the wild, you should respond by making yourself look big and scary. Gasping for breath like an asthmatic in my underwear with untied tennis shoes probably didn't fit the bill. Nevertheless, I continued on with determination.

I made it to a grassy clearing when my pounding heart and tired lungs forced me to stop and catch my breath. I stood there, doubled over with my hands on my knees, and saw a thin creek running alongside the trail. Some kind of tropical bird chirped angrily at me as it sat perched on a limb. I then began to look more closely at the bird and recognized the bizarre color pattern on its wings. I had been chasing this bird for half a mile.

Feeling stupid, but relieved that it wasn't a ghost, I headed back toward the house. Just as I started back, my foot smacked into something solid. I kneeled down to see a rice bag with a concrete block stuffed inside. There was some kind of Japanese writing on the side.

"Only on the Island of Ted," I coughed out.

Although the moon provided a trickle of light through the trees, my fears began to surge again: it was very dark and I didn't exactly have a clear path home.

"Am I really alone out here?" I wondered to myself irrationally. My steps became more urgent as I pushed through the bamboo leaves. Fear drove me forward and I began to run with the distinct feeling that someone was chasing me. I ran for more than a half mile and was not at my front porch yet.

I was hopelessly lost.

At that moment I was frozen with fear. There were sounds in the distance, almost human. I was losing it.

It wouldn't be daylight for several hours and I was out here alone. A light wind tickled my skin and I heard that familiar, and eerie, sound of bamboo trees swaying back and forth. To keep control of my senses in this dark, unfamiliar forest, I thought back on the many films that had scared me as a youth. Then I brought to mind all of my experience producing similar films, which always took away the creepiness factor. I knew the blood was fake and the knives were made of rubber. Likewise, I knew I was alone out here and nothing could actually harm me.

After another forty-five minutes of roaming around the forest, I saw a pin point of light in the distance. It was my porch light. As my foot hit the entryway, a peal of thunder rang out and the sky began to spit rain.

"There is a God," I thought with a grin.

Rain thumped against the glass door leading to the deck. I toweled off in the bedroom and reached for a little hatbox that had been stashed under the bed. I pulled out my elementary school yearbook and flipped to my picture at age ten.

Geez, I was a dork.

As the memories came flooding back, I flipped a few pages forward and saw a charming picture of Heather, the girl of my young dreams. Beside her picture, penned in fading blue ink: My future wife!!!

"Well, well… we meet again."

I flipped the yearbook shut and reached inside the box. Next up was a coffee-stained promotional mug from one of the earlier films I'd produced. After that was a group photo with Roger and a few actors. Then my fingers found it—*the letter.* The words seemed to float across the page:

…regret to inform … body found near Juarez … identified as Theodore LaSalle, Sr … our sympathies go out to you and your kin …

I folded the letter and stashed it inside the box. It wasn't a time for that kind of reminiscing; I wanted happy memories. I grabbed the next item—my college diploma.

Summa Cum Laude—Bachelor of Arts

My father had wanted me to study philosophy but my own twisted sense of pragmatism saw such a field as more useless than fine arts. To be fair, my immense fiscal gains were more accurately the result of knowing a guy who knew a guy who knew Roger Graham. The degree meant nothing. That's how the film business works: everything is predicated on relationships. Passion and talent are a bonus, but hardly necessary if you know the right folks.

The next, and final, item inside the box was a crumpled homemade Christmas card I'd made for my parents when I was six. Written in crayon were these words:

To the best Mom and Dad on the Planet! I love my new hat!!

That one got me. My stinging eyes began to glaze over and I stashed the box back under the bed. It was time for sleep. I hit a button on the lamp to dim the light and watched rain-streaks run down the glass door. That night I dreamed about a neck massage.

CHAPTER

20

A loud crash! I sprang out of bed, wobbled a bit, and found my shoes. Dashing toward the dock, I saw Nako trying to steady himself on the front of his boat, which was caught in a slow-speed tail spin.

"I can't tie off! Wind is too strong and dock gave way! Sorry about damage!" he shouted.

"Don't sweat it," I said.

"Here—catch!"

Nako began tossing several small boxes at me on the beach and we formed an impromptu assembly line. After the ninth box, Nako gave me a military salute and went back to manning the wheel. I returned his salute and waved him goodbye. It was good to see him again. I wanted to talk but he was in a rush. Oh well.

I spent that evening in front of the tube watching Korean dramas. Since they run these in the Philippines, English subtitles were provided—sort of an in-between method of communication. For that reason, some of the subtitles were humorously incorrect and that reminded me of this fad I heard about that is presently affecting the Korean youth culture.

Apparently it's hip to wear t-shirts with random English phrases on the front. And by random, I mean random. Like "Bomb Crush!" and "City Slinky Collector."

These shows, however, were surprisingly entertaining and had me laughing and engaged the whole time. "My Girl," starring Korean cutie Lee Da Hae, was my favorite.

An oldie but goodie, my father used to say.

Watching the actress' charming antics really made me miss the pursuit of love—*badly*.

"Boy, do I need to get out of the house," I thought.

I spent the next several days hammering wood beams to repair the broken dock, aided by a large collection of do-it-yourself books housed in my study. Staying busy really helped to stave off the loneliness. However, on my twenty-eighth day on the island, I was happy as punch to see Nako's broken vessel on the approach. He was my only source to the outside world, so I'd been singing along with the radio every day to keep my voice strong enough for conversation, if one should arise.

Nako smiled and gave a "thumbs up" to acknowledge my handiwork on the dock. He tied off the boat and dropped his anchor before going below deck to fetch a few boxes. This time he was able to help me carry the boxes up to the front porch.

"You know," he said. "I think you bought up entire supply of Pop Tart on mainland."

"Can I ask a favor, Nako?"

He looked at me with caution, thinking that perhaps I was about to request something absurd.

"What you need?" he asked in a low pitch.

"I was just wondering if you wanted to hang out for a little while. I'm rather bored."

"You play baseball?" he asked, far too excited for his age.

Nako carried a couple of baseball gloves and a few balls with him wherever he went. We spent the afternoon playing catch in the wet rice field until the sun began to set and the mosquitoes emerged.

"I miss this much about Japan," he told me. "Here they all play hoops. I tall for Japanese but never like that game. My father teach me baseball."

"Same here. Lifetime Cubs fan."

"Ah… Chicooga."

I nodded. Close enough.

After baseball, I introduced Nako to the world of fine wine and amused myself by watching him get lit. We sat in front of the tube and laughed at Monty Python until our eyes watered. Nako seemed fond of attempting to give out sage wisdom while under the influence. He noted the frequent commercial breaks by pointing at the TV with his empty glass.

"Ted, you see these product? They all is crap! You spend hard earn money and find out they not as advertise. They junk! Really such junk!"

"You might want to back off the booze, pal."

He smiled for a moment, and then his face turned inquisitive. After a slow blink of the eyes to get his visual bearings, he looked at me.

"Ted, why you here?"

The question caught me off guard.

"I'm sorry?"

"Why you here?" he repeated, words slurry. "Where your family?"

Boy, did this guy know how to sober up a party fast.

"I don't have any family, Nako."

"How you not have family?"

"I just don't. Never married… never had any kids. I'm an only child."

"Your parent?"

"Dead."

"Oh no. That make Nako very, very, very, very sad. What happen them?"

I sighed, not wanting to open that can of worms, but Nako's drunken gaze was persistent.

"My mother died young. Cancer. My father was a missionary in Central America. He was just traveling in a car, heading over a ridge, and the driver took a sharp turn off a curve and…"

I stopped, feeling a sudden burst of emotion.

"Anyway—long story short, he didn't make it. The driver lived. He went there to build wells and a hospital and died preaching to a bunch of superstitious peasants. And that's the story."

I didn't mean to answer him so sharply but the pain of that moment flooded me like a tidal wave. It was a senseless way to end one's life, or so I had reasoned. I sat there, fuming, and stared at my hands for a long, sobering moment.

Then I heard Nako snoring and looked over to see him sound asleep at the end of the couch. At that moment, I had to laugh. This drooling Japanese cargo boat operator, with no ability to hold his liquor, was now my best friend. It was either profound or profoundly sad. Still, Nako had ten times the integrity of Roger or Jerry so perhaps I was moving up in life.

The next day I bid Nako farewell to avoid getting him fired for missing too much work. For the next week I spent much of my days watching Korean dramas and drinking coffee on the veranda while looking out over the terraced rice field. For about three seconds, I considered fasting from all electronics for a month but, not being much of a Luddite, I realized that my techno lust was the only thing that kept me from feeling too lonely on still nights.

Living a life of solitude was something I was committed to and being realistic about the pitfalls helped my decision considerably. I knew it would get lonely and that was the price. So be it. I was lonely in Chicago too. Besides, there was always Lee Da Hae and those wonderful Korean dramas to keep me sane. God bless those corny television writers.

CHAPTER

21

"What was that?" I wondered aloud in a weak voice, peering up over the deck railing.

It was a cloudless Saturday morning. I had now been on the island for forty-nine days. I was sitting on the veranda with a cup of steaming black coffee when I saw movement in the weeds, near a pathway that leads into the bamboo forest. I stood erect and strained my eyes. There it was again!

Swearing that I had seen a human face, I ran toward the spot where I had seen movement.

"Hey!" I yelled out in a cracked voice. "Stop!"

Knowing I was more than likely chasing a bird or a lizard didn't matter. There was no feeling of embarrassment on the Island of Ted, so shouting to animals was pretty much the norm.

I blasted up the pathway and into the forest and then slowed down as I approached a faint knocking sound. It grew louder and louder as I tiptoed forward into the clearing.

THWAK!

I grabbed my chest; my heart pounding. I froze and beheld a startling sight ten yards in front of me.

It couldn't be.

An eleven-year-old boy sliced open a coconut with a large machete. I shifted my weight a little and the rock beneath my foot slipped. The boy looked up at me sharply and we just gazed at one another for what seemed like a full minute.

"Who are you?" I asked.

The boy began looking around for an exit. He was visibly uncomfortable.

"How did you get here?" I pressed further.

Was this my imagination?

The boy suddenly took off into a full sprint, racing into the forest. I remained still in a daze, just watching him go.

• • •

Back at the house, I paced back and forth with a satellite phone to my ear. I was furious.

"I already told you! This was part of our deal!" I shouted into the phone. "I am calm, but you have to do something about this. There's a little boy and probably an entire family living on my island!"

I felt like throwing the phone through a window, but wanted to replace neither.

"I don't know how they got here," I told my agent, who was probably cowering on the other end. "I want them gone yesterday. I can't tolerate squatters on my land, stealing from me."

After an apology from the agent, I thanked him and hung up. Immediately, air sprang from my lungs and I doubled over in a violent cough.

I felt something warm on my fingers and looked down to see patches of red.

"I just coughed up blood," I said in a state of sedated panic. Talking to myself didn't make it less scary.

I reached for a glass and filled it with water from the sink. The glass became blurry as it neared my face and my head began to feel very warm. Sweat was forming on my forehead. THIS WAS SERIOUS.

I spent the next hour trying to get a hold of Nako before he finally returned my call.

"What took you so long, Nako?" I shouted. "I'm dying here!"

I heard laughter at the other end of the phone.

"I'm serious. I'm coughing up blood for crying out loud. Wait—where's that?"

• • •

I sat on the stern of Nako's boat sipping some green tea he'd brewed for me. It tasted like warmed-over garbage.

Nako was cooking something on a little battery-powered burner. Out of his pot came vegetable broth, which he poured over a wooden bowl of starchy noodles.

"This make you better until we arrive."

I chewed on a few noodles with the chopsticks he'd handed me and slurped on the salty soup. It was actually pretty relaxing.

I watched Nako go back to manning the wheel and said, "This is the first time I've been off the island since settling in. Feels strange."

"Time away is good," Nako said, sounding like an ancient proverb.

"I already miss it," was my response.

Nako smirked, perhaps wondering from which planet I had escaped.

"I call ahead," he told me. "Got you appointment tonight. We'll dock in Surigao shortly."

Nako tried to read me with his eyes.

"You find that boy yet?" he asked.

"No," I said. "Little asshat stole my coconuts. But I called Yano… he's taking care of it."

Nako laughed from his belly in a way that was beginning to irritate me.

"Your real estate guy? That Yano? Don't count on it."

"Why's that?"

"He lazy. Sorry I tell you now. Is true."

"Great. Well, if that kid is still there when I get back I'll put him on a raft and send him sailing myself."

Nako shook his head.

"Why you so mean?" he said.

"I'm not mean. I just want to be left alone."

He wasn't buying it.

"I can't really explain it," I said defensively. "Isolation kind of sucks but it's still more appealing to me than socializing with idiots. You know how scared I was this morning when I thought I was going to die? But what scared me even more was the feeling that I'd still prefer this life to any other. Loneliness only hurts when you run out of distractions."

"You very strange man, Ted."

"My destiny is to be alone. I don't need people."

"Okay. I stop boat here and you swim to shore."

Nako just shook his head again, not sure how serious I was in my state of delirium. As for me, I meant every word. That's exempting emergency medical care, of course. Nako was a good friend and deep inside I knew he liked me too, and not just because I paid him for his time. We had become actual friends.

I could see city lights through hazy fog as we neared the Cebu docks. The harbor was filled with a massive cruise ship, a few commercial boats and a smattering of fishing vessels. The intense coughing had calmed a bit, but I was still worried. You don't yack up blood for no reason. Nako patted me on the shoulder and then stood up and dropped his anchor.

• • •

I sat in a lime-green concrete room with chipped paint while Nako smoked a pack of cigarettes outside the building. After a long wait, a male nurse entered the room with a clipboard.

"Your result is clean," he said.

"I don't think so. I'm dying."

"Sorry to inform you of this but you will live."

"Then why am I coughing?"

"Environmental allergy, more than likely. This is common in Americans."

The nurse laughed and shook his head at me before handing me a bottle of pills.

I met up with Nako on the sidewalk outside the clinic. A group of young, college-age ladies stood on the opposite corner, staring at me while smiling and teasing one another.

Nako looked at me and said, "You dying?"

"Unfortunately, no," I replied.

"Good. Let us celebrate with those Pinays over there."

Nako pointed to the group of girls and one of them shouted to us across the street.

"Hey, Joe! Wanna party?"

I gave Nako a weary look.

"I just want to get back as soon as possible," I moaned.

"Come on, man. Chick here love American. Your white skin help me catch girls."

"I'm tired," is all I could offer.

"Okay then," he said, disappointed. "You the boss. My very grumpy boss."

The noise of the city was deafening and the streets were far too crowded for my taste. A loud motorcycle whizzed past and missed my leg by an inch. I guess Nako was used to city life and probably saw his bi-weekly boat trips to the Island of Ted as a break from the monotony. He mostly ran cargo trips throughout the archipelago but only stopped at busy ports. My little homestead served as a brief escape from the rough seas and bustling harbors. He thanked me by playing baseball for a couple of hours every other week.

CHAPTER

22

Nako was dead-on about my agency contact, Mr. Yano. A week later, I still had no response from him. At night I heard strange things coming from the other side of the island but it could have been my imagination. Who was that kid? Why was he taking my coconuts? These thoughts lingered as the days wore on.

I'd occasionally stand on the roof deck with binoculars to spot the occasional boat or cruise ship. It was one of the games I played to entertain myself when I grew tired of satellite TV.

I spent a great deal of time working out as well. Push-ups on the bamboo floor and crunches on my bed every morning before coffee—it was my routine and done by rote. It occurred to me that maintaining physical strength could come in handy, even if one chose, like me, to live in confinement. Who knows, right?

The Spanish hit these islands in the sixteenth century and the Japanese tried to finish the job in the 1940s. It was, in fact, American troops who liberated the islands during World War II, and that's something not forgotten by

Filipinos. To this day they have a high level of affection for all things American. A very average-looking guy in the States would be treated like a rock star over here. He could even date girls who were, in reality, way out of his league. This affection also goes for Europeans and Australians, since Filipinos have trouble discerning their accents. Like I was told when I entered the country, if you're white then you're American—end of story.

I spent the afternoon walking through the forest since nothing was on TV and there was a nice sea breeze. My internet connection had gone down during the night and still wasn't up, so traipsing around my property sounded like a good idea. The island itself was much bigger than I had expected, based on the photos I was given on the mainland. Even still, the amount of foliage was enough to obstruct much of the view. I would break a good sweat just getting back to the ocean where my little home-built dock sat, awaiting some of Nako's attention.

It occurred to me that I hadn't worked on my screenplay since I'd been on the island. Maybe that could keep me busy for a while. So I sat down at the computer and started a new scene.

INT. HOUSE—NIGHT
Warren poured himself a scotch and imagined a life where he wasn't so lonely.

I stared at the screen, which was now a commentary on my own life, and then highlighted the text and hit DELETE. Maybe I'd find my story later. After all, I wasn't exactly in a rush.

It was early in the evening. I stood on the dock and watched the gentle tide when from out of nowhere, a familiar noise hit my eardrums. I turned and saw the little boy walking along the tree line! He was holding two coconuts and didn't notice me.

"Hey!" I shouted in full throat.

He quickly darted out of sight and I took to running, this time in very loose flip-flops. Nevertheless, I was gaining on him! He may have been small and fast but I had the advantage of longer legs. He would have to face me this time and answer my questions.

Maybe the kid was raised by wolves or something. Didn't matter, because he still had to go.

As I ran, the twigs and branches whipped across my upper arms and gave me little micro-cuts, the kind that sting but don't bleed much. I ran like my life depended on it, jumping to clear a fallen tree without missing a beat. After a quarter-mile, I slowed to catch my breath, then went back into a full dash.

My heart was pounding so hard that I felt it throbbing against my chest cavity. Sweat poured from my head and my lungs burned like they were filled with boiling water! Still, I continued my pursuit, always keeping the boy in sight.

After running after this kid for what felt like a good two miles, we reached a clearing and he took off, full steam, down a subtle embankment. When I crested the hill I stopped in my tracks.

"What the…," I said, trailing off.

I had ran all the way to the southern end of the island. On the beach sat fifteen makeshift nipa hut cabins, built with bamboo trees and banana leaves. It looked like the remnants of a an abandoned tourist site.

"What the hell is this?"

There were at least twenty or thirty people, all Filipinos of varying age and gender, strewn about the beach. The kid I had been chasing was immediately tackled by another boy his age and they wrestled around a bit. He then jumped back to his feet and grabbed the arm of an older gentleman. The boy pointed a finger in my direction. Not knowing what to do, I walked down the embankment and was met by a friendly handshake, which I ignored.

"Hello, sir. My name is Rene," said the older gentleman.

"I don't care what your name is. That boy is stealing from me. Who are you people?"

"I'm very sorry. We didn't know someone live on this island too."

"He knew," I said. "I've been here for over four months. My house is on the north end. This island belongs to me. He stole from me before."

I was still out of breath, struggling to make due. Rene turned to the boy.

"Manny, give this man back his coconuts."

The kid picked up the coconuts and brought them over. He dropped them at my bruised feet.

"His birth name is Manuel but we call him Manny after the boxer Manny Pacquiao, because he's a scrapper. I'm very sorry about this," Rene said.

I suddenly felt badly for the kid, but was still in shock and a little irritated.

"Never mind. Just keep the coconuts. I want to know why you are here on my island. No one is supposed to be here."

"We are from Mindanao," Rene said. "We arrive here by boat three weeks ago."

"Three weeks?" I repeated with disdain. "Where's your boat?"

"We don't have any boats. The government put us on a ship and drop us here. We only had time to bring few items each."

I turned my gaze on the others and saw two men whispering to one another about me. Their faces didn't look friendly at all. I began to swell with anger and stormed toward a small mound of sand where I waved my arms to call everyone to attention. On this occasion, I had no problem with public speaking.

"Everyone! Trespassers! I want you to hear something. My land, which I paid for with my own efforts, is not your barbecue pit. You do not belong here."

I scanned over the crowd, particularly eyeballing the two men who were giving me threatening glares.

"I don't care how you arrived," I shouted, "but know this: You have to go. It is not optional."

I jumped down from the mound, turned back toward the trail and began walking toward the clearing. Behind me, I could hear them engage one another in a foreign tongue.

Glancing back over my shoulder, I saw a worried group forming. The two men with the bold stares were up in arms, yelling at Rene. The older man made some "calm down" gestures and, to my surprise, they obeyed him. When the two men turned their sights back onto me, I faced the forest and continued onward.

I spent that evening once more reminding my real estate guy why I'd requested this island in the first place. Squatters would not be permitted. This is a big country with plenty of islands. Whoever dropped them onto my shores had, whether intentional or by random chance, made an epic mistake. They are squatters from Mindanao. That's great. They can go back there.

I plopped onto the couch and almost broke the remote in half when I grabbed it. I needed to calm down before my blood pressure shot up even further.

CSI. Re-run. Great. I flipped channels, landing on an old favorite: BBC World News.

Uh oh. I leaned forward.

At the bottom of the screen, a news string began to crawl:

"Relief sent to Mindanao… President Aquino asking for foreign aid…"

I flipped to the local news feed from Manila and caught the full story. A female reporter said something in Tagalog and then a homemade videotape filled the screen.

Two ten year old kids were playing near a fruit stand as the camera tried to become steady. The kids waved to the camera just as a CAR EXPLODED behind them! The camera was knocked to the ground as frantic people ran through the streets. Then sirens. Dead bodies and human limbs could be seen from the sideways image behind a cracked lens.

"Holy hell!"

My heart fell into my stomach. I felt like I'd just seen something that could never be erased from my memory— just like the news report that broke Delores' fatal accident. Only this time I saw a dozen lives taken right before my eyes, including a group of happy Filipino children.

I turned up the volume as the reporter began speaking in English, as they often did when dealing with serious news stories.

"Military is still being sent to the region along with Red Cross in an effort to return stability. Mindanao residents are now uneasy about the violence that struck an all time high one month ago when a church bombing killed dozens of families. Many have fled to other regions of the northern and western Philippine islands."

I reached for the phone.

"Yano, it's Ted. Hold off on doing anything just yet. I need to check some things out. Goodnight."

Something was different. A tingling sensation shot up my arms and I felt my body growing more numb by the second. What was happening? I wanted to retch, to rid myself of this feeling, this foreign invader. My vision grew cloudy and the sting of tears wet my eyes.

I reached for a bottle and poured a drink. But throughout the night, even as the glasses began to add up, the awful feeling in my gut remained. I couldn't get the poison out of me. It was two in the morning when I finally staggered upstairs and into my bedroom. I fell back against the sheets and let them wrap around me in a silky embrace.

Then I slept.

Part Two

"One of the hardest things in life is having words in your heart that you can't utter."

-James Earl Jones

1

PHILIPPE NUDGED HIS brother. "Look... it's that asshole again."

"Where?" Jose replied.

"Up there. On the hill. He's been watching us for a while."

"I don't trust him. He thinks he's better than us."

It was just after nightfall when Ted stepped into the clearing and saw the south beach village aglow from the light of a bonfire. Children danced around, playing with sticks they had fashioned into play swords. Various adult Filipinos sat about, eating from wooden bowls and drinking water from coconut shells. The pale moon was large in the sky, casting a serene glow over the beach. To Ted, it didn't even look like the same island. Over here it was so... alive.

Ted's gaze landed on a beige Red Cross tent to the east of the village. A pretty Filipino woman in a white doctor's lab coat was talking to Manny. Her silky black hair was pulled up in a bun, threaded with a chopstick and a stethoscope hung from her neck. She looked to be in her late twenties and had a radiance about her that was very attractive. She touched Manny's nose and he ran off to play with the other children. The woman's eyes then moved across the children and a smile emerged on her face. Ted couldn't take his eyes off this mystery woman. She was intoxicating.

"What is your story?" he asked the night air.

The woman's gaze then broke away from the kids and she looked toward the hill, directly at him.

Ted panicked and spun around, tried to walk away, then stopped. He was busted. She had already seen him. He turned back around to make eye contact with her but she was gone. His eyes searched the beach and found her at the bonfire, speaking to Rene. She pointed up toward the clearing where he stood.

"Great. Wonderful."

Ted let go of a lengthy sigh and made his way down the dirt path to meet them on the beach. Several villagers turned, watching him curiously as he approached. Some of them staggered back, bracing for another rant. Philippe and Jose gave one another a look. *Here we go again.*

Rene quickly walked out to greet him wearing a giant, warm smile. A true diplomat.

"Hello, sir! I hope we have not disturbed you."

"You're still here," Ted replied, groggy and reluctant.

The old man offered a firm handshake once more.

"I spoke to Manuel and he promised not to take your coconuts again."

"How about I make a deal with you guys. If I allow you to stay here for a little while, can we agree that no one breeches my property?"

"Yes, sir."

"I mean… for any reason at all."

"Yes, sir."

"It's just that I'm a very private man and would appreciate it a great deal if I could remain that way."

"Yes, sir. I will tell the others."

Ted's gaze drifted over to the woman in the doctor's coat. She stood near the bonfire and was curiously gazing back at him. The children began tugging on her medical coat and she spoke to them softly in their native language.

"Is that your daughter?" Ted asked Rene.

The old man looked in her direction and smiled.

"Oh, no. That's Lanie. She came from Manila with few medical people. They left short time after but she stay. I think she has no family, only her work."

"Well, I'm going to get back," he said. "You guys just stay over here on this side."

Ted started back toward the path and felt his conscience pricked. He stopped walking, turned his head and offered a half-hearted smile. "By the way… I'm Ted."

• • •

He sat at the computer at midnight, hand cupping his chin. Chilled coconut water sat in a glass beside him. He wanted to get cracking on the screenplay but nothing would come out. He stood and walked over to the bedroom window and peered out over the back of the property. He unlatched the door, letting it fall open—perhaps thinking he could hear what was happening on the south beach. But he only heard crickets and a breezy wind buffeting through the banana trees.

Ted reached for his satellite phone and dialed Nako's cell.

"Bossman! What you need?"

"Nako, can I ask you for a favor?"

"Shoot."

"Can you bring me something a little different next time… along with the usual?"

"Depend. What you need?"

Ted couldn't believe what came out of his mouth next. "Toys."

"Like what?"

"High tech. Videos games. Whatever. And a box of solar chargers."

"Lucky for you, I just arriving in Tokyo. I use your regular charge card?"

"I trust you, Nako," he said with reluctance.

"I know, boss. Me too."

Ted spent the next few days wondering if this was the right thing to do. Was he doing it for them or for himself? Did he have ulterior motives? These were questions he didn't think he'd ever ask again after leaving the States. But he figured these people wouldn't be here much longer so what was the harm?

2

SEVERAL DAYS LATER, Ted moved down toward the
south beach village, carrying a box on his shoulder. A group
of Filipinos were in the water with bamboo fishing poles.
The plastic-covered door to the Red Cross tent was open
and he saw Lanie inside, wearing that ever-present white
medical coat. She was reading a book, never once looking
up to see him.

The children, who were playing in the water, saw the box
he was carrying and ran to him. Lanie saw the sudden
commotion and looked up as Ted began handing the kids
hand-held video games. Rene waved at him from across the
beach. Manny was smaller than the other kids so he got
pushed out of the way and was last in line. He stood there
quietly, with his head down and his hand outstretched. Ted
handed him the video game.

"That's called a Nintendo DS. I used to have one back in
Chicago."

"Sorry I take your coconut, Mr. Ted."

"I'll live," Ted replied.

"Thank you for the game."

Manny then ran back to play with his friends, all of whom were busy trying to figure out how the games worked. Rene approached Ted with a few of the others.

"Thank you for bringing the toys. Or as we say here in Philippines, *maraming salamat*!"

"I won't even attempt that."

Rene turned to the others.

"This my wife, Lynette and my nephews, Jose and Philippe."

"Nice to meet you all."

Jose and Philippe wouldn't make eye contact with Ted. He sensed a bit of tension and saw Rene quietly nudge Philippe, who turned and left. The younger man didn't seem to care for small talk.

Ted looked over toward the medical tent and saw Lanie observing them. Her eyes quickly went back to her book and Manny noticed him swooning. Ted made a fist gesture and Manny returned a goofy smile. The kid knew.

Ted had been told that Lanie was Filipino but her face contained traces of something more mysterious and exotic, perhaps French or Portuguese. The villagers had built a bonfire at dusk and Ted sat down on the beach, eating some of the fruit they'd given him. Manny plopped down beside him, full of energy.

"You're a very fast runner," he said. "You almost caught me in the woods."

"I ran track in high school."

"I'm the fastest one here," he continued. "Even the older kids can't beat me."

"You like to run?"

"Mr. Ted, can I ask you a question?"

"Um… sure."

"Do you like Dr. Lanie?"

Ted nearly spit out his food.

"What? Who? Did someone tell you that?"

"I saw you look at her. She's so very pretty."

"Well, not that I noticed but she's okay," he replied skittishly. "So I'm not… no. I don't like her that way. In fact, we've never spoken."

"You know, Filipino girls are different from American," he said. "At least the ones I met in Mindanao."

"Yeah? How so?"

"Hard to explain. My English is not so good."

"Your English is better than mine," he added.

"Not Lanie," Manny said while shaking his head in exaggerated fashion. "She from very small village before she go and study in Manila. She might be smart but she struggle with English."

This kid was beginning to fascinate him.

"You know," he said. "When you speak to Lanie you should tell her 'Mahal kita.' It will impress her that you know that."

"Hey, I never said I was trying to impress… how do you say that again?"

Manny began to enunciate, "Ma-hal. Ki-ta."

"Ma-hal. Ki-ta?" Ted clumsily repeated.

"Very good."

"What's it mean?"

"It means 'Nice to meet you' in Tagalog. That's her language. Say that when you first talk to her. She will like it so much."

Ted began to repeat those words under his breath several times before deciding to give it a shot. Ordinarily, approaching a complete stranger was not an idea he'd entertain, but this was different. The girl would be gone soon enough, so engaging her in polite conversation didn't carry much pressure at all.

• • •

One of those old-school kerosene lamps burned inside the medical tent so Ted figured she would, at least, be awake. His stomach groaned nervously, much to his surprise. *Why the sudden case of nerves?*

He stopped in the doorway of the medical tent and observed Lanie eating a piece of fruit while flipping through a magazine. He just watched her for a moment. Her arms moved with feminine elegance. Big, brown eyes glistened in the dancing light. The scent of coconut sunscreen wafted toward him.

Lanie looked up, startled. A long, awkward silence fell between them as they watched one another, waiting for the other to speak. Not a good start.

"Mahal kita! I'm Ted."

Her eyes widened suddenly and she quickly turned her head away. Ted was confused by what appeared to be a rather cold response and figured he had probably said it wrong.

"Mahal... kita. I'm Ted."

This time he was careful to enunciate properly. She still wasn't responding and, instead, kept her eyes on the bottom corner of the tent.

"Sooooo," he said in a nervous tone. "Rene told me you're a doctor."

Lanie glanced up at him but he couldn't read her expression. Her face was a mixture of embarrassment and annoyance. He pointed toward the magazine on her little cardboard table.

"Oh, you read National Geographic?" he said for no reason whatsoever. "Good taste. I enjoy a good periodical myself."

Lanie just stared at him. After a brief moment, she again turned away. Same expression of annoyance.

"Well, it was nice to meet you," he said. "I live on the other side of the thing... my name is Ted. I'm Ted. It's what people... call me."

Lanie kept her silence, refused to look at him.

Ted dipped his head, embarrassed, and stepped out of the medical tent feeling like the biggest idiot on earth. *Am I now repulsive to women on an international scale? Why was she so quiet? Did I offend her?*

Ted heard Rene and his family laughing around the bonfire so he decided to join them. He sat down beside Philippe, who was roasting a banana over the flame.

Rene looked at him and said, "Ted, are you enjoying yourself here?"

"It's been fun. Listen… what does 'Mahal kita' mean?"

Lynette clutched her heart and then leaned on Rene's shoulder with a romantic grin.

"It means 'I love you' in our language," he said.

"I'm sorry?"

"Where did you learn Tagalog?" Rene asked.

"Good lord," Ted sighed under his breath. "Manny was teaching me. I think I just said that to Lanie. Maybe twice."

Several of them gave him a sharp look. Then silence. The group then erupted in laughter.

"Man, he got you good!" Rene cackled.

"What a little punk. And after I gave him a DS too."

"You know, Manny has a crush on Dr. Lanie. He's a smart one."

"I just wanted to introduce myself," he admitted.

Philippe physically pulled back at this.

"Ah… then you say 'Kamusta ka?'"

"What's that mean?" Ted asked. "I'd love to fondle you?"

"Fondle? No, that is proper greeting in our language. It mean 'How are you?'"

"Kamusta ka?" he repeated.

"You got it now, Romeo."

Ted knew he couldn't leave things so incredibly awkward between them so he worked up the nerve to approach the tent once more. Surely things would go better this time around. *They couldn't go any worse.*

• • •

Ted knocked quietly this time before entering the medical tent. Lanie's eyes darted around to see if he was alone. She appeared very uncomfortable.

"Kamusta ka?" he said.

A subtle interest flashed across her face, her eyes gently engaging him. Her reply was very soft. "Mabuti. Ikaw?"

"Oh... uh... I don't really..."

She then began a flurry of conversation that took him by surprise. The girl was talking a mile a minute and he had no idea how to respond to it all. From the look on her face, she must have been sharing an inside joke with him. Her voice was soft and feminine, almost child-like. Combined with her flowing words of mystery, Ted was held captive, afraid to interrupt and prove himself an even bigger idiot.

Her eyebrows lifted, as though she'd finished all that by asking a question. Ted panicked. He was loath to respond for fear of making her quiet again.

"Ok lang? Ano?" she asked.

Her eyes narrowed, that familiar look of annoyance once more surfacing.

"Um… one second," he stalled.

Lanie seemed puzzled as he fled the tent in a hurry.

In his days of producing movies, Ted had grown very accustomed to pressure. At times, he thrived on it. Yet, for some reason, at this moment in time… he panicked. And ran. Memories of Heather and Teresa bombarded his mind and he ran all the way home. A single thought remained with him. *Even here? Seriously?*

Even on this island so far from civilization, this nest of tranquility, Ted once again felt the rush of infatuation and knew exactly how it would end. Badly.

Rene and the others at the campfire looked back at him curiously as he rushed toward the clearing. The older man's face bore serious concern. He hopped to his feet and made his way over to the medical tent, where he disappeared inside, closing the door behind him. Philippe and Jose began to murmur, hiding their conversation from the others.

• • •

Ted spent a few days resting. Due to heavy amounts of unforeseen running during the past week, he'd developed a serious case of soreness in his lower body. And something else was bothering him. Since that first interaction with Lanie, life at the mansion felt different. Perhaps it was knowing that he was no longer alone on the island, or maybe it was the fact that his embarrassing history with women had followed him here, but he felt anxious all the time now.

He watched movies on television and laughed at stupid cats on YouTube, but the quiet moments were the worst. She was all he thought about.

Back in Chicago and LA things were easy. He was a fast-talking, successful movie producer with a fancy house and a customized luxury car. Women also threw themselves at him—the wrong kind of women. His father used to say, "Never marry a girl your mother wouldn't want as a daughter."

That narrowed the search quite a bit. But there was a problem: Ted only knew how to talk to Hollywood girls. The normal, down-to-earth types, scared him. The ones who actually had something interesting to say, or an educated view of the world, left him speechless and clumsy. He had no idea if any of that applied to Lanie but it sure seemed like he was back to being a bumbling idiot. The moment the girl engaged him, he ran.

Who does that?

Romantic pain was no stranger to him, and neither was a bottle of expensive wine. He uncorked and went to town, getting blitzed. Ordinarily, getting hammered for the sake of getting hammered was only a societal compulsion. These days, it really took the edge off. A danger, however, did present itself in times of drunken stupor. You do not want to talk to the woman of your dreams in that state, despite the false courage brought on by fermented grapes. Ted knew this well and bolted the doors, just in case. While drunk, he had a devil of a time opening doors—especially locked ones. In a way, it was much like engaging your car's child locks to prevent sudden escape. So with six glasses of pinot noir behind him, he reclined on plush Italian leather in the den and drifted away.

3

A TATTERED BASEBALL, which had clearly seen better days, sailed over mature rice stalks and landed in Ted's mitt. In no time, he snatched it with his free hand and sent the ball sailing across the field, where his smiling companion braced for a catch. Nako was still reeling from an earlier moment of levity.

"Man, that kid got you good!" he said. "I want to meet him!"

"Not that it would've mattered," Ted shouted to him. "My experience with American women should have trained me for this. It's just not meant to be."

"Some things follow you around, huh?"

Ted caught the ball and held it.

"What's wrong?" Nako wondered out loud.

Ted was quiet, caught in a moment of reflection.

"This girl," he said. "This girl is something else. I've been around A-list actresses and not one of them, in their finest hour, could match her charm. I'd sell my kidneys to be with a woman like that."

"Both of them?"

"I'm telling you, she's different."

"Your five-second conversation tell you so much," Nako said, heavy on the skepticism. "I thought you want to be alone? All by yourself?"

Ted took an honest pause to sort through the very real dilemma Nako had just highlighted. Was the loneliness and isolation finally wearing him down? Was he ready to abandon this whole enterprise, just because he'd fallen for some mysterious beauty who, for all he knew, felt only repulsion toward him. Their first two encounters were not exactly friendly.

"I do," Ted replied. "Of course I do. It's just… I can't explain it. I'm confused."

"You know, there's a saying in my country."

Ted, knowing his friend's lack of poetic skill, braced for the worst.

"What's that?"

"Try and try until you die."

"That's incredibly depressing. Thank you."

"It doesn't rhyme like that in Japanese," Nako admitted.

"You're like the Japanese Yoda, man."

Nako caught the ball and sent it back.

"This Yoda? Is good thing?"

"Yeah," Ted told him. "It's a compliment."

Ted spent that evening pacing in front of the television while biting his nails, which, by that point, were more like nubs. The words of Japanese Yoda bounced around in his head until he decided that it was time to give it another shot.

"If I'm going to fail," he reasoned, "I'm going to fail epically. Go down in flames. Let it be."

Ted knew that he'd spent time swooning over Teresa only to find out that the road was a dead end. He figured that Lanie would surely reject him, and may have already done so, but this time it wouldn't take months or years to find out the truth. He would just deal with the hurt and move on. After all, he'd chosen a life of solitude for a reason—and he had not forgotten it.

4

TED MOVED THROUGH the darkness with his ever-ready flashlight as he approached the south village. Kerosene lamps lit a few of the houses and some of the kids were still playing on the beach. Relaxing a bit, Ted just watched them for a moment. He then turned his attention to the medical tent; the journey made him feel tense, but alive.

He knocked his fist against the fragile door.

Lanie glanced up sharply, recognized him through the plastic window. Ted faked a couple of coughs and Lanie lifted the door's latch to allow him entrance. He noticed that her medical coat was torn on one side.

Speaking more slowly than usual, he said, "Do you always wear that thing?"

Ted pointed to her coat and her eyes followed. She actually understood him this time. Lanie looked back up at him with eyes beautiful and searching, full of mystery.

"Mosquitoes," she said in a soft, controlled tone.

"Oh, so it protects your arms?"

"Yes."

Ted nodded and smiled. Lanie cautiously smiled back, still uncertain about this strange American in her tent.

"So I just came by because I have this cough," he told her. "It's pretty bad sometimes."

Ted pointed to his throat.

Lanie removed a stethoscope from her pocket and circled to his back. She lifted his shirt up while turning her head away innocently.

"Malamig na?" she asked.

Ted looked back over his shoulder.

"Is cold?" she repeated in English.

"No, it's fine."

Lanie lowered his shirt and moved the stethoscope to his chest.

"Make deep your breath," she said.

Ted drew in a deep breath. Then another.

"Salamat," she said. "Oh… that's 'Thank you.'"

She put the stethoscope on the table and wrote something in her notepad.

"Is it bad?" Ted began to actually wonder.

Although he'd faked his cough to see her, he had not forgotten a certain incident involving blood that had sent him to a clinic on the mainland.

Lanie turned around and motioned for him to stick his tongue out. She then stuck a wooden spoon in his mouth to suppress his tongue and clicked on a small flashlight while looking inside.

"We're moving a little fast here," he tried to say without moving his tongue.

The joke was dead on arrival. No response.

Lanie clicked the flashlight off and scribbled something on her tablet.

"You have the malaria," she said in a serious tone.

Ted's jaw dropped to the floor.

"Holy hell," he thought.

"But I…," he sputtered. "How can that even…"

Ted then noticed Lanie smiling at him.

"It's joke," she said. "Ted, you have some allergy?"

Ted exhaled and let his shoulders drop.

"Dust?" he asked, already knowing the answer.

"Mosquito."

"Hmm. Surprising." And he meant it. "Thanks for taking a look. What do I owe you for your trouble?"

Lanie looked at him as if she didn't understand.

"To pay you for the visit," he enunciated. "How much?"

She waved her hand at him dismissively.

"Are you sure?" he asked.

"Take this."

Lanie handed him a can of mosquito repellant.

"To protect you."

Ted was oddly moved by the gesture. It was her only can.

"Listen," he began. "Is it okay if I ask you a personal question?"

"What this means?" she asked in a soft voice.

"As in… do you have a special man in your life? Like a boyfriend, I mean."

Ted felt strange saying the word *boyfriend* to her. He had already studied her hand for a ring and hadn't found one.

"I don't belong to anyone," she said with a hint of caution, eyes growing less friendly by the second.

"It's hard to believe that someone like you is not already taken."

"Ano? Like what?" she said fast.

"No, because you're very pretty. And I just… shit. I'm saying this all wrong."

Lanie looked away from him. Her eyes were back to the bottom corner of the tent. She pushed her hair back over her left ear. Ted didn't know if she was embarrassed or upset with him.

"I'm sorry."

"You are kano, yeah?" she pressed.

"That's right."

"American guy is so forward."

Her tone sounded irritated.

"I'm sorry," he said, his face turning three shades of red. "Listen, I didn't mean to bother you. I don't even know why I…"

Ted's voice trailed off and he felt ashamed. Lanie saw that he was embarrassed and said, "Filipinos not like that. It's a more… how you say… timing thing."

"Timing?"

Now Ted was the one confused. He saw that she was struggling to find the right words to use.

"I mean… it's hard to translate into English."

"I'm sorry." Ted offered.

"Relationship here is delicate."

Lanie looked down with a loud sigh. "I'm not using right words. Ted, you are nice guy. The kids like you. But I'm not American girl."

"You're not interested," Ted said, almost to himself. "And now I feel stupid for bothering you."

"What you mean?" she said with a bit of frustration in her voice.

Ted sought cover now. He inched toward the door. He had walked into this girl's world and forced her into an awkward moment.

He opened the door halfway and said, "I just wanted to give you a compliment. I don't even know why. I just saw you and… felt something, like I needed to talk to you. But that's… not… I'm sorry to bother you. I really am."

He saw that Lanie was trying to comprehend what he was saying but his mouth wouldn't stop moving.

"I mean—I came here because I wanted to be alone. It's not like… even if you… never mind. I'm a mess and if I keep talking like this I'll sound even crazier. Not that you can understand any of this but… well… goodnight."

"Bye, Ted," she said in a soft, confused voice as Ted was already halfway out of the medical tent.

Standing alone, she sighed to herself.

"Ay naku."

• • •

Ted sat at his computer in the bedroom, typing up a frenzy. A sudden spark of creativity had caused him to fire up the screenwriting program once more. After two hours, he had already churned out thirty pages. On the screen now sat:

Warren's advances toward Lanie were thwarted when she picked up a steak knife and rammed it through his chest.

Ted smiled a bit, then deleted the sentence, replacing it with:

Warren knew that winning the girl's heart would take an investment. Then again, she would be gone soon. He had nothing to lose.

Ted then underlined *nothing to lose*.

• • •

The rain had petered out by the time Ted left for his early-morning jog. Along the trail he found Manny, sitting alone on a log and playing with his Nintendo DS. Manny looked up from his game and began running alongside Ted, wearing a big grin.

"What's up, kid? You know I told my friend Nako how you burned me."

"I'm sorry, Ted. I just don't want her to like you. She's my girl."

"Dr. Lanie is your girl?"

"Yeah," Manny said. "But she's maldita."

"What's that?"

"In English it's like... snob, I guess."

"Really? She doesn't seem like a snob to me. A little hard to read, perhaps."

"Oh, she nice. But maldita too."

Ted laughed at the kid. He found him amusing and blunt, like himself.

"But I'm not stupid, Mr. Ted. I know she's so very old for me."

"What are we saying here?"

"I know how Filipino girl thinks."

"You're going to help me gain the interest of Dr. Lanie? I'm pretty sure she hates me just a little bit."

"Maybe, but I can help with that. There's a condition," he said. "I want some more game for my Nintendo."

"It's a deal."

Ted offered his hand and Manny gave him a grown-up shake. It was cute.

"So how do you plan to court her?" Manny asked.

"Court? Who am I, Bill Bixby?"

"You must court a Filipina. You can't just ask them for date because they think it makes them cheap."

"So what do I do?"

Ted's interest was piqued. He knew well the irony of taking relationship advice from an eleven-year-old but these were desperate times.

"Before you ask a girl out you have to court her for a while. Give to her flower, gift, letter... things like that, until she accept you for a date."

"Oh, so that's what she meant," Ted said out loud. "Um... look, I'll bring you some more games next week. Thanks for your help."

"But hey," he said. "If it don't work out between you and Dr. Lanie can you put in a word for me?"

"You're a wild one, Manny."

Manny gave him a sly wink. Ted began to turn back, then stopped.

"Hey, you want to watch TV?"

Manny's face lit up.

"Go ask your dad. Hurry up."

5

_____

TED AND HIS young friend munched on junk food as Cartoon Network blared from expensive surround sound speakers. Ted's house was like Disneyland for a kid.

"So how long is this courtship thing supposed to go on?" Ted asked during a commercial break.

Manny guzzled his soda.

"Depends. Father said he court my nanay for more than one year before she accept a date."

Ted's eyes turned into grapefruits. "What? That's crazy. A year?"

"I guess it's normal for courtship."

Ted reclined back on the leather sofa, knowing he didn't have that kind of stamina. Besides, he thought, Lanie wouldn't be on the island much longer.

"So what kept your father going? I mean, what if, after all that time, your mother had rejected his offer?"

"I ask him that too. He say that love is sacrifice."

"Tell me about it," Ted thought.

His intense, and sudden, feelings for Lanie made him cautious. Being an introspective man, he knew well the dangers of intense attraction whether physical, emotional or both. The only safe bet, though painful, would be to let her know soon that she was being courted. He made the mistake of waiting with Teresa and would not do so again. However, he also knew that coming on too strong would be a bad move so this would be a dance of subtlety and finesse. If it still ended badly, he reasoned, at least it would end quickly and Lanie could head back to Manila not giving him a second thought.

• • •

Lanie sat down at her makeshift desk with a roasted banana. She had just finished hanging a mosquito net over the block of wood she called a bed. She was a woman of simplicity and had an innocent beauty that almost made her glow. Her father, equal parts Japanese and Filipino, had also practiced medicine among the poor in Manila before he died in a random stabbing. Her mother was a Filipino dressmaker with Scottish and German blood. The result of their union was a girl who could have easily enjoyed a career in modeling but, rather, decided to follow in her father's humanitarian footsteps.

The camp on the south beach was always festive, though a solemn prayer-time was conducted each morning at the stir of a handmade wind chime. Ted heard that sound as he stood in the clearing. A gentle fog rested among the huts under an orange smear of sunlight. The strong scent of salty ocean water caught his senses as the wind chimes danced in his ears. From afar, he watched them gather and kneel prostrate in the sand.

Ted knew from his research that Filipinos were deeply spiritual and mostly Catholic, but he had never seen this kind of worship anywhere. These people were not on their faces to grovel before an angry God but looked more like survivors pulled from deep waters onto dry land, and that's exactly what they were: a band of refugees who were thankful for every breath they took.

Ted looked on, wishing his father could be standing there with him to see such a sight. He felt a strong urge to show someone these Mindanao refugees bowing to their creator on a misty beach at sunrise. "It's one of those sights you carry to your grave," he thought.

Mindanao was a large, war-torn island to the south of Cebu. A faction of militant terrorists called Abu Sayyaf made the local news every so often by setting off random bombs around metro buildings and transit stations. They lived among the villages in small holdouts that protected them from the US military, which had partnered with Filipino troops in the region. The US was mainly there to train an underfunded local task force and assist with aid. But their efforts were often undermined by the jungle terrain— one that proved advantageous to the indigenous, machete-waving Abu Sayyaf, who rolled into town on dusty Jeeps and wore scarves over their faces.

Ted watched these saints of Mindanao kneel in the sand, lifting up their prayers to heaven like burning incense rising upward. Lanie was among them. She wore that familiar white jacket, hair pulled into a ponytail, loose bangs hanging over her eyes like a silk hijab veil. Her tanned face was wet with tears.

Lanie wiped her bangs back over an ear and rose to her feet. She smiled down at Manny, who always flocked to her like a chick to a mother hen. They joined hands and she spun him around like a carnival ride. Ted wondered if Manny had told her about their conversations, and kind of hoped he had. But a new fear now plagued him: what if Lanie were to accept his offer of courtship? Would he and his cynicism eventually wear on her and choke the life out of this poor girl? And would it be worth abandoning his chosen path of isolation? How would her presence change things at the house?

"I'm getting ahead of myself," he thought.

Ted motioned Manny over and handed him an envelope that looked like it had been torn open, then re-taped.

"I need you to put this inside Lanie's room when she's not there. I wedged a note inside so hold it upright."

"Aye aye, captain!" Manny replied with a salute before running back down the hill with the envelope in all manner of direction. Ted just shook his head.

• • •

Nako spun the baseball on the tip of his glove, then popped it up into the air and caught it behind his back. Ted applauded the effort and then ran to the far end of the rice field to make his catch. He returned to home base a little out of breath.

"She read it yet?" Nako asked him, teasing.

"I don't know. I sent it over with Manny two days ago. Haven't had the guts to go over there."

"I will have to meet your friends sometime," Nako said with a big smile.

"Yeah, speaking of which… thank you for bringing those extra items," Ted told him.

"No worry," said Nako. "They easy to find."

• • •

Light rain fell on the south beach village. No one seemed to be around. Familiar lantern light dotted the insides of the bamboo houses. The door to Lanie's tent was open but Ted saw no one as he passed by. A gray fog rested over the beach, making it feel deserted and eerie. Suddenly, a noise. Then faint singing.

Ted walked the beach for some time and noticed a small point of light coming from inside the trees. He moved toward it carefully. A stick crunched under his foot as the voices grew in volume.

Ted stopped outside of a large tent that had been erected near the edge of the forest. The saints of Mindanao were inside, holding candles and singing softly. Through the plastic tent window, Ted watched them sing with tremendous joy in a language he barely understood. His eyes scanned the huddle of people before resting on Lanie, who stood in a corner. Her eyes were filled with a beauty that surpassed the physical. This woman, who could seem solemn and yet jovial in the same moment, further intrigued Ted. It was hard not to stare at her.

Philippe stood near the edge of the tent, miming the words, but hardly singing. To Ted, it seemed like the man wanted to be somewhere else. Philippe just had a different energy than the others, and his eyes were always full of this controlled rage, ready to snap at any moment. Ted backed away from the tent, careful not to make any noise.

• • •

Lanie walked back to the south beach with the others and saw Ted standing outside of the Red Cross tent. He pretended not to notice her as she approached, coy as ever.

"Oh. Hi there," he said.

"Are you waiting me?" Lanie asked.

Her face was hard to read.

"No, not at all. Yes."

Lanie gave him a tentative look and the hint of a smile. Ted held out a flower. Her eyes narrowed a bit, not sure how to take the gesture. Ted began to withdraw his arm slowly when she reached out and took the flower. She put it to her nose and sniffed.

"Is nice flower," she said. "Thank you."

"Did you get my letter?" Ted asked.

"Yes."

"Did you read it?"

Lanie gave him a look that could only mean: *of course, you idiot!*

"Okay then," he said. "Enjoy your evening."

"Bye, kano."

Lanie entered the medical tent and saw a gift box on the table. Her hands caressed the box as she began to untie the red ribbon. As it fell to the sandy floor she opened it and looked inside, a sudden wave of unexpected energy coursing over her. Her hand moved to her trembling lips. Inside the box sat a brand new medical coat, neatly folded, pristine, white as snow. Stitched on the breast pocket, below the collar: Dr. Lanie.

She took a moment to collect herself, deeply moved by the gesture. Her tiny hand moved to her face and wiped away the sudden arrival of tears. Lifting the coat out of the box, she noticed that another note lay at the bottom. She removed it and read it silently:

You give me hope. Hard to explain. Your friend, Ted

A thump at the door. She turned sharply. "Kano?"

But it wasn't Ted. Philippe appeared in the doorway, eyeballing her with his focused gaze. "Looks like someone is being courted."

Lanie grew quiet as he moved toward her. Philippe then sat down on the makeshift medical bed.

"He's up to no good. I'm just trying to help you."

"He's a nice guy," she said.

"They tell me he's a billionaire. That he has houses, and girlfriends, on every continent."

"I wouldn't know," she said. "Go ask him yourself if you're so interested."

"Lanie, I know you're an innocent girl but this Ted guy is a kano. They only come to places like this for one reason. To pick up local whores."

Lanie physically pulled back. "He came here to be alone. He's not some playboy."

"If that's true then why is he giving you gifts and flowers? His story doesn't add up. He says he came here to be alone, but he doesn't act like it."

"Unless you have a cold or need stitches, I'd like you to leave."

Philippe shrugged innocently. "By the way," he said, "I know about your little secret."

Utter surprise leapt onto Lanie's face.

"I know the truth," he warned. "I was there. Maybe Ted deserves to know too."

He then smirked and walked out of the tent, leaving Lanie alone with her troubled thoughts.

6

_____

TED SPENT THE next week resisting the urge to visit the south beach village. Lanie knew he was interested and that was enough for now. He felt a strange peace about the whole thing and resigned himself to the couch, where he ate copious amounts of popcorn while immersing himself in more Korean pop culture. He knew well the addiction of those sappy dramas but was already in too deep.   Each show had the same recycled hero and heroine. There's always a stoic, rich Korean guy with Anime hair who is all too mean and hostile toward the simple girl under his employ until he discovers, by episode 10, that he's actually in love with her. Each of the Korean dramas were some derivative of that basic storyline, and it never got old to him.

• • •

The golden sun raked across Ted's property, an emerald rim of light glowing atop the palm trees. He stepped onto the concrete patio at sundown and remembered why Hollywood folks call this "magic hour." In LA it lasts about twenty minutes and hits right before sunset. It's that last moment of daylight before night takes over, and it's the best time to shoot a scene. Many Hollywood films shoot their most tender moments at this time of day because of the soft glow that wraps around the actors. Though likely an exaggeration, he'd once heard that director Terrence Malick shot an entire movie at magic hour. Shooting for only twenty minutes a day can wreak havoc on a production schedule!

It was on days like this when Ted missed being a movie producer. Or perhaps the nostalgia came from being so far removed from the industry that its warts no longer showed. But he did love the thrill of stepping onto a set and always got a rush when the lights were struck and cameras were moved into position.

Ah, the glory days.

Ted had been on the island for less than six months but it seemed like an eternity. He wondered what might happen when the Mindanao saints packed up to return to their homeland. He wondered if Lanie would reject him like all of the others. He even wondered if his affection for the girl was real or just a whisper of the former life he renounced before stepping onto an airplane and giving his finger to humanity.

He was a man of mixed emotions and only wished that the magic hour, with its warmth and perfect beauty, could remain. But before he even finished that thought, the sun had set and night sprang forth. The crickets began their serenade and Ted walked back inside, the darkness at his back.

7

LANIE SLEPT ON the wooden cot in relative comfort. Filipinos often slept on hard surfaces due to necessity but it afforded them certain advantages, like healthy backs.

She awoke from her slumber and heard something knocking against the frail tent door. She yawned with a cat-like stretch and pulled it open. Manny smiled at her mischievously, the look of a used car salesman.

"Kamusta, Manny. Magandang umaga," she said, which means, "*Hello, good morning!*"

"Are you busy, Dr. Lanie?" he asked.

"Hindi, Manuel. Just sleeping."

Manny danced around like children always do when they want to say something but lack the necessary social timing.

"Okay," he said. "I only come by to ask for you walk on Ted."

"Ano?" Lanie said, meaning, "*What?*"

Ted then appeared behind Manny, smiling with embarrassment.

"Walk *with* me, Manny. Not *on* me."

Manny shrugged. "It's all the same," he said, not seeing the humor. He hit Ted with an energetic high-five and ran off to play with the other kids.

Ted looked at Lanie and asked, "Are you free?"

She hesitated, then turned back inside the tent and returned with a small tote bag.

Ted was relieved that the girl was willing to take a walk with him, but it also made him nervous. They were slowly making headway on the language issue, finding a delicate balance between broken English and bodily gestures. It was cute, and oddly effective. And as Lanie loosened up, her English seemed to improve as well.

• • •

They walked along the much treaded dirt path through the bamboo forest. For the first time, Lanie was not wearing her doctor's coat. Ted had learned a few Tagalog phrases the night before but decided he'd rather not try them out. He might end up proposing to her by accident, or calling her an unflattering animal. They walked for a while in silence and neither seemed to be bothered by it.

"Have you ever seen snow?" he asked, randomly.

It took a few moments before Lanie responded. Ted thought perhaps she was translating the answer in her head before speaking.

"I see that before, yes," she said.

"Really?"

"Yes," she said, a mischievous look forming on her tanned face. "I saw in the movies."

She smiled. It was the first time Ted had witnessed her trying to be funny since telling him he had contracted malaria.

"You need to visit Chicago. We get quite a bit."

"Ted, can I ask?" she said, out of nowhere.

"Sure."

"Not to be a nosy person, but I feel on your back is knife wound?"

They stopped walking. Ted wondered if he wanted to go into all the gory details. He was afraid the silliest little thing would scare her away.

He took a deep breath and said, "I was robbed."

Lanie didn't understand his words so he made a finger gun to illustrate. She seemed to catch on.

"Stabbed by someone I was trying to help," he said. "Ironically, it was snowing at the time."

"It still hurts?" she asked.

"Only when I cough."

"Can I ask?"

"Anything."

Lanie hesitated a bit. Ted knew she was having a hard time finding the exact words.

"You have a person there to worry for you?" she asked with a voice so soft it was hard to hear.

"No… no, I don't," he said. "But I might have a person here. Who knows?"

Lanie punched him on the arm. It hurt.

"You would lie to someone sweet as me, kano?" she said with a hint of sarcasm.

Ted saw in her a strange confidence mixed with cute insecurity. It was a playful energy that was getting less and less awkward as the minutes wore on. They walked along at a slow clip, just enjoying one another.

Ted had so many questions for her but didn't want to come off as obtrusive. He needed something safe. "Where did you go to school?" he asked.

"Ano?"

"University. Where did…"

"Ah, in Manila. School here is hard. Our exam is difficult compare to Stateside."

"Someone else told me that," he said, trying to think of whom.

"Is true. Very hard to complete your studies here. And you need foreign sponsor for the cost."

"Did you work during university?"

"Yes!" she said, exited. "I serve drink to tourist."

Lanie grabbed a smaller tree by the trunk and gave it a shake.

"Move!" she said, gently pushing Ted out of the way as three coconuts fell from the heavens.

She grabbed one of the them as Ted sat down on a log to observe. Lanie struggled to crack it open with a jagged stone she had found nearby.

"Hey, don't hurt yourself," he said. "You're the only doctor around for miles."

"Hey, kano… I'm city girl," she countered. "This how they do in my place."

The third swing cracked the coconut down the middle. She twisted it to make two separate halves and handed one to Ted.

"See," she smiled, "giving drink to tourist again."

"I see what you did there. Clever"

"Is easy with machete. For professional like me, is only just rock. Baby coconut is so very sweet, right?"

"This tastes amazing. You know, I've gotten pretty handy at whacking these myself. They're all over my property."

Lanie looked up from her coconut smoothie with big eyes.

"I'm sorry to ask this. I know what you said. But… may I see it?" she asked with a child's enthusiasm.

TED LED HER to the clearing with a full view of the rice terraces and Ted's massive house in the middle. Lanie's eyes scanned across the land, taking it in.

"Your rice need harvesting."

"You know how to do that?"

"Of course," she said, a bit concerned for him.

"Consider me impressed. Let me show you the pad."

"Pad?" she inquired. "This what we call when helicopter put on hospital roof."

"Well, you could probably land a chopper on mine too."

Ted and Lanie walked through the rice field, stalks snapping as they moved past.

At the house, they entered the foyer and Lanie immediately removed her shoes. Ted had forgotten how other cultures always remove their shoes out of respect for the homeowner.

"It's so big for you."

"I enjoy my space," he said, a bit too defensively. It did seem absurdly large to him all of a sudden.

"So what your occupation back there?"

Ted took in a long breath.

"I talked banks into loaning my company money to make overly expensive movies, and then talked actors into thinking the script was right for them, even if it wasn't. Often times I doubled as a glorified secretary for a boss who didn't appreciate me nearly enough and every so often I'd attend award shows and watch Roger get credit for my own brainchild. When that wasn't happening, I was cashing very big checks and avoiding people."

Ted noticed Lanie looking at him and realized he had gone off on a tangent. The girl had no idea what he was talking about. She turned her eyes to the entertainment system.

"That pay for all this?"

"Well, I invested most of it and got lucky. Kind of worked out for me."

"It's exciting, your job?"

"I mostly sat in front of a computer. Or at airports."

Lanie nodded. She didn't find ironic humor very funny.

Changing the subject, Ted asked, "So what do you do for fun? I mean, when you're not helping sick people?"

"Oh, I love the cinema. My auntie teach us English using American movie. You know Sound of Music?"

"Of course."

"As a girl, I watch that million times. I wanted to be Von Trapp kid."

"You wanted to be hunted by Nazis?"

Lanie gave him a strange look.

"Want to see upstairs?" he asked.

He led her up the steps and into his bedroom. Lanie looked around with wide, playful eyes.

"So beautiful in here," she said. "It look Chinese."

"I designed this place from a short story I wrote in college. It was a fairy tale but—"

Only at that moment did it sink in…

"Not so much any more," he confessed. "Now I'm a real life cartoon character."

Lanie pushed the door open and walked out onto the bamboo deck. The breeze lifted the strap from her shoulder and she crossed her arms gently before pulling it back. Ted watched the graceful way she moved and found himself staring at her. He noticed that she looked cold from the strong breeze so he positioned himself behind her innocently. She turned.

"You are rich guy?"

"That's kind of relative."

"Can I say something?"

"Of course. Yes."

"I'm sorry," she began. "I find rich people usually so unhappy. This true?"

He broke eye contact with her and looked away. She had a way of cutting to the chase and Ted, in all his years of schmoozing, knew only how to beat around the bush when it came to heavy topics.   "Rich people, poor people… I find that most people are unhappy," he replied.

She just looked at him, searching his face. "And you?"

He shrugged. "Depends on the day. Some are better than others."

"Coming here to Philippines—this help you to be happy?"

Ted rested his weight against the railing, giving himself a moment to reflect on what was fast becoming a very serious, and unexpectedly deep, conversation.

"I honestly don't know yet. It's not exactly what I had imagined."

"So what you imagined?"

"Swimming in the ocean. Spearing fish and roasting my catch on the beach. Getting swept away by great literature with nothing to distract me. Ever. Fresh coffee on the veranda, Mozart and crickets escorting me to bed. Writing to dull the ache, and the occasional glass of red wine to sweeten the quiet nights."

She bobbed her head, taking in Ted's patchwork of a dream. "And this not your life now?"

He had to smile. "I've swam in the ocean once, broke my Mozart CD, settled for instant coffee, live with constant writer's block, and that occasional glass of wine usually becomes a bottle. Or two."

"The literature?" she asked.

"That became Korean dramas on TV. And don't even ask me about spearing fish. For that, I have Nako. And his catch usually ends up on my six-burner gas range, which is quite far from the beach."

"So sad," she said with a smile. "So what you think of me, kano? Give your impression right now. Don't lie."

Uh oh, this was heading for trouble.

"I find you extremely curious," he said honestly. "But I can't say I understand why you're doing what you're doing. You could make a lot of money in Manila or even in the States. But, you're here. Working for free. Why?"

Lanie looked at him like the answer should be obvious. "We are from different worlds, kano."

Her tone was soft and non-judgmental but Ted felt a sting. He smiled to hide it.

"I know," he offered, meaning it.

Lanie brushed past him and sat down on the bed, playing with his oversized pillow.

"Why you're not married?" she asked.

Ted turned to face her with his hands tucked inside his pockets like a frightened little boy.

"I've always had trouble finding the right one. Actresses or LA bar sluts are an easy pull. But down to earth girls— not so much. They seem to require a certain quality that's missing in me."

"You have some skill, no? In talking?"

"I just always say the wrong thing, you know, like asking a woman her age."

Lanie, confusing that for a question, jumped in. "I'm twenty-nine this year."

It took a moment for Ted to see what was happening. He decided to just go with it.

"When did you graduate?" he asked.

"I finish high school by age fifteen. Then my bachelor at nineteen, masters at twenty-two and doctorate was two years ago. I did residency in Manila, then small clinic in Mindanao. Now here, doing more volunteer for experience. I want to be the best."

Despite her broken English, Ted was not dealing with a lightweight here.

"And you?" she asked innocently.

"Just a... liberal... arts... degree," he said, his voice trailing off. "An art degree."

"Oh," she said while nodding her head to be polite. "But you put to good use."

Ted found the sight of this brilliant, exotic woman sitting comfortably on his bed to be utterly strange. This was his oasis of solitude and now he was staring into the eyes of a woman so fascinating that, for a moment, the idea of wanting to be alone felt utterly absurd to him.

"So what is your age, kano? You looks old."

"Mid-thirties. But who keeps up any more?"

Lanie nodded toward a framed picture on his bed stand.

"That is your parent?" she asked.

A sudden chill moved up his arms. It was as though all of his senses were being assaulted in a moment's time. He could almost see his father's face, standing there near the base of the stairs, watching Lanie and him talking so casually. Ted could imagine Pops swelling with pride, a subtle grin on his face that said, "You did good, Son. She's a real keeper."

"Dead," he told her.

"Oh," she said softly. "Must be hard thing for you."

Ted shrugged his shoulders. She noticed that he was suddenly withdrawn and said, "I'm sorry. That's very personal question."

"No, it's fine. That was a long time ago."

For a brief moment Lanie thought about opening up to him about the death of her own parents but decided against it. This relationship, or whatever it was, was still too new. No point weeping on shoulders just yet.

She started in a gentler voice, "Thank you for the gift. And letter."

"Oh, that. It's no big deal."

"Well, is big deal to me," she said. "We Filipinos don't forget a kindness."

Ted felt so vulnerable around her, and now more than ever. Lanie had no pretense and didn't know, or care for, the art of subtlety. To make matters worse, she also came with Doogie Howser-type credentials. In reality, she was far more out of his league than the Teresa he longed for in his days at Graham Entertainment.

Lanie stood.

"Come on," she said. "I cook something for you. Local food. Good for cheering up my new kano friend."

LANIE SEARCHED THE fridge for anything resembling actual food. Ted was a man of simple tastes, for the most part, and ate the same things every day. He watched her trying to hide judgment as she sorted through the odd choices in his sparse cabinetry. It was like she didn't recognize a thing.

"You have no food?" she asked.

"I stick to the basics."

Lanie poured a capful of coconut oil into a hot saucepan, along with butter and cinnamon. She coated a banana with brown sugar and tossed it in the pan.

"You will like fried banana. Must better than your Poppy Tart thing."

Ted smiled and replied, "You speak blasphemy."

They sat on opposite ends of a glass table. Lanie unfolded a napkin and placed it in her lap. Ted took a bite and washed it down with cold milk.

"This is good," he admitted. "You make me want to plant some banana trees."

She raised a thumb toward the window. "You already have that."

Ted bobbed his head and smirked. What kind of dunce can't cultivate his own land? The girl must have seen him as some spoiled idiot who would likely starve while surrounded by bounty. The ocean outside teemed with fish, but he couldn't catch one if his life depended on it. His forest produced several types of delectable fruit, and yet he desired boxed pastries.

"You cook a lot?" he asked, feeling more inadequate than ever.

"I cook for my grandparent when I was younger. At university I serve in the kitchen as working student for some semesters."

Ted was beginning to learn the art of being blunt and knew Lanie would not be someone to easily take offense. He was curious about so much but didn't want to overwhelm the poor girl with questions.

"Are we friends?" he asked to test the waters. "I mean... we're becoming friends, right?"

She set her plate down and looked at him with curious eyes. "Ah. My friend Ted has a question for me, no? He's nervous to ask something of this silly girl sitting at his table?"

He grinned wide. "Fine. Why does your hair smell so good?"

She looked at him funny.

"I know that's a weird thing to ask but I noticed it when we were standing out on the balcony."

Her hand covered her mouth as she hid her laughter.

"No, no," he said. "I'm not trying to be funny or whatever. It just seems difficult to groom oneself in a place like this."

"We use a soap, Ted. And shampoo. You maybe hear of these items?"

"You bathe in the ocean?" Ted asked her with a hint of disgust on his face.

"Our shower is pale of water. You take ocean and boil it. Then when it cools you pour it over your body."

Ted was speechless.

"Someone is pampered?" she teased.

"Not at all," he lied. "I've done the bucket shower thing. When I was three."

Lanie just shook her head in amazement. *Rich boy kano.*

• • •

Ted walked her back to the tent as it neared late afternoon. They stood at the tent entrance for a moment without talking before he waved goodbye and left. Several villagers stood watching them from afar. Philippe brushed past her, then froze as Ted disappeared up the path.

Philippe sighed. "You should tell him, Lanie. "

"Mind your business."

"It's not right."

"You say anything to him and I'll bust your face."

Philippe cackled. "You're the one hiding secrets."

"It will ruin him, Philippe. You can't say anything." She looked down at her hands. "And things have changed."

"Have they?" he said skeptically, then walked away from her.

It was nearly impossible for Ted to think about anything except Lanie as he walked the trail back to his concrete mansion. He made a quick sandwich and sat in front of the TV with his clicker. Taking a bite of sandwich, he flipped to Telemundo and caught the tail end of a Mexican soap opera.

An olive-skinned man in a poncho grabbed hold of a lady wearing a red evening dress and said, "Why didn't you break my heart when you had the chance?"

She looked up at him with a sparkle and responded, "Love is a sacrifice, Raul."

Ted knew just enough Spanish to catch that line.

Love is a sacrifice.

Ted quickly stood, ran up the stairs, tripped and fell. Then bounced back to his feet and sprinted for the bathroom. He looked around for something, knocking items off the counter. He found a bottle of cologne and doused himself with no fewer than ten squirts. He ran a comb through his hair and reached for a toothbrush. Ted was determined to make his move before the night was over. Why waste another minute?

10

THE SOUTH VILLAGE was quiet and the beach empty.
Ted stood in front of Lanie's tent wearing a pair of black
jeans and white button-up shirt, collar flared open. He
looked nice but smelled like a brothel. Soft music could be
heard inside the tent. Lanie stitched a shirt with a needle
and thread. An old battery operated radio sat in front of her
on the table. She looked up and saw Ted outside the door,
waiting for some kind of invitation. He waved and entered
the tent looking very shy. Lanie quickly hid her handiwork,
stashing it inside of a purse.

"Is that for me?" he teased.

"A surprise for my new friend."

Ted looked at her a little too long. He caught himself and
diverted his eyes. *Play it cool, old boy.*

She wiped her bangs behind an ear and said, "I guess
someone is bored, no?"

"No," he said. "I just wanted to see you. Nice radio."

It obviously wasn't. An old cassette tape rattled off an
Eric Clapton tune: "Wonderful tonight."

"Is that your tape?" he asked.

"Yes, my own. I like ballad music. Makes me so calm, like falling in love."

"So you're a hopeless romantic after all, waiting for a prince to arrive."

"When you find him," she said, "tell him I'm here in the medical tent."

"Will do," he replied with a smile.

Lanie, with no regard for self image, began to sing the lyrics. She may have found a couple of actual notes but it was only by accident. Ted was amused.

"Okay—that's quite enough. My ears might start bleeding."

Lanie gave him a goofy grin but remained beautiful beyond words, even while unkempt and playful.

"Hey, listen—that's too good a song to waste. We need to do something about this."

Ted offered Lanie his hand.

"Dance with me."

She pretended to think it over, then slowly took his hand. Energy shot through his body, that magic tingle of first touch. She reached over and grabbed the radio.

"I warn you," she said. "I'm very good dancer."

"Good. I'm not."

          Palm trees swayed under moonlight as a peaceful tide rolled in. The old radio sat on a mound of sand as Lanie and Ted slow danced, arm in arm, alone on the beach. This, alas, was the prom dance he never got to have.

It occurred to Ted that very minute that whatever else was going on in the world, this was all that existed. This beach. The warm night air. The stars overhead. The sound of the ocean and its thick, salty scent. The cheap radio. And this girl.

He could smell the coconut nectar of Lanie's hair as her head sat on his shoulder. Ted knew he was dancing with a woman who was foreign to him in more ways than one. He was lost in time. Lanie moved her head to his chest and sniffled quietly. A tear swelled and fell onto his shirt.

The song then tattered out before ending in a slur. They continued dancing for a few seconds without music.

Lanie wiped her eyes and said with a laugh, "Dead battery."

Ted released her and wondered why she was crying. His heart ached.

"Sorry," she apologized. "My father dance this song with me during my debut. When Filipino girl turn eighteen her parents throw big party and she wears a special dress. I'm just having some memories."

"Your father…"

More tears fell and her face twisted with pain. Ted fell silent. He knew.

He touched her cheek with his thumb and gently wiped her face. She moved her head back reflexively and he felt out of place. An awkward moment. Lanie smiled to let him know everything was all right.

"I'll have Nako bring you some new batteries on his next trip."

"Thank you, kano." Her voice was soft, almost a whisper.

Ted tried to read her face but Lanie kept her eyes down. They stood like this for a moment.

"I guess it's late. I'll get back."

"Goodnight," she said.

_____

11

IT WAS ALREADY late in the afternoon when Ted and Nako decided to conclude their ritual of tossing the baseball farther and farther each session. The Japanese man was so enamored with Ted that he began showing up once a week to hear more about how things had been developing on the island. He also liked the conversation. Spending endless days and nights out on the sea took its toll.

They snaked around the property and found bamboo chars on the back deck. A good place to rest. "I saw a shark last evening," Nako said. "He follow my boat for several meter so I give him food."

"What did you feed him?"

"Rice noodle soup. He enjoy it."

They sat on the stoop and Ted reached into a cooler and offered his friend a chilled bottle of water.

"How your friends?" Nako asked.

"Aside from Rene and a couple others, I get the feeling the villagers don't like me very much. They see me as some idiot kano who wipes his ass with hundred dollar bills."

"So what you use, twenties?"

"So much for friendship," Ted replied with a grin.

"How things with the girl?"

"Complicated."

"How that?"

"She's great, but we're getting kind of close. Feels strange to spend time with a female who isn't trying to get something from me. I feel like I can actually trust her."

"So why your tone is sad?"

Ted shrugged, gazing at the tree line. "You should see how she takes care of those kids. I mean, she said her dream is to work with Doctors Without Borders for crying out loud."

"Ah," Nako said, catching on. "So staying on Island of Ted not her dream."

"Not even close." Ted swigged from his bottle.

"But if she your girl, you can travel with her."

Ted held his tongue.

"What you so scared of?" Nako pressed.

"Let's review: Her goal is to run around to war-torn countries and stitch people back together. I bought an island. You do the math."

"You would not give up dream to be with her?"

"Our dreams aren't even in the same hemisphere." Pointing to the ground, he said, "This was a lifetime in the making. I've always known that I was meant to be alone and I've spent a fortune to solidify that reality."

Nako was soft in his reply. "So the girl has change that?"

Ted looked down at his hands and said, "I wish I could say yes."

"I think you just afraid that you wrong."

"About what?"

"Afraid that you need other people in your life, boss. And just you… is not enough."

Ted smirked. Lately he'd been thinking of the peaceful nights and the lack of complications that drew him to the island in the first place. He thought of Lanie, how she had responded to him in a way that was surprising and yet, somehow, felt just right. But it was getting too real. He wasn't used to real. His world was not hers and that bothered him.

The magnetic draw he felt toward her was offset by the reality that moving forward with Lanie would tear apart everything he'd been working for. Sure, the loneliness would vanish, but so would his hard-fought independence. Ted would now be responsible for loving someone else and tending to her needs, and not just his own. The thought scared him.

Lanie was not someone he could just put aside whenever he got bored. She was not a television show that he could switch off with the click of a button. She was flesh and blood and he loved her. He loved her so much it hurt when thoughts of her entered his mind.

Ted was torn. He had fallen for a woman who threatened to steal everything he'd been working for. But she was real. Her affection for him was also real. And that complicated things.

"I feel like such an alien sometimes."

"Technically, you are alien."

Ted laughed. He needed to laugh.

Suddenly, a loud clap of thunder boomed from the heavens. Ted jumped so hard that he spilled his drink, at which Nako chuckled and stood up.

"That sound my cue. I don't want to get caught on a wave."

Nako slapped Ted five and turned toward the dirt path.

"Nako!" Ted shouted.

He noticed that Nako was still wearing his mitt so Ted grabbed the baseball.

"One more! Go long!"

Nako raised his glove near the bamboo forest and Ted let the ball fly. It sailed clean over Nako's head.

"I said go long. That's not long!"

"You going to pay for that one!" Nako responded as he ran through the trees to fetch the ball.

He finally spotted the ball in a clearing. Snatching it off the ground, he rose to his feet with caution. Nako's eyes drifted up toward the western sky.

Ted wondered what was taking him so long. Nako then appeared from the tree line, a worried look hanging from his face. His steps were fast as he approached in a hurry.

"Something wrong?" Ted asked.

"I need to get back."

"What's up, old man?" Ted teased. "You tired?"

"Storm clouds. Looks like a big rain is coming."

Nako's face had changed to a mask of concern.

"Keep an eye on news channel," he said.

Ted gave him a thumbs-up and Nako saluted his friend before heading back. Ted ducked into the house and uncorked a bottle. Once the spirits hit his lips on that very first sip, he knew what he would choose. The epiphany struck him without warning, and yet he knew it would be the right choice and not some sudden impulse. Everything clicked neatly into place, confidence warming his chest as the wine traveled down. He just needed to tell her. His gaze fell to the kitchen window, where he saw darkness overtaking the land. Things would be different in the morning.

12

TED FOUND HER on the beach early the next morning. She was reading to Manny on the sand, the wind catching and lifting her coat tails every so often. The boy laughed hysterically at something she said and fell over onto his side. Lanie slapped him on top of his head with the book and then tickled him. They rolled around in the sand and then Manny sprinted off toward his cousins, who were calling to him from the water. The children splashed around in the vast ocean with gloomy gray skies overhead.

Lanie caught her breath and stood. Ted waved his arms through the air in exaggerated motions. She spotted him in the clearing, a curious and surprised look on her face. She jogged over to meet him near a fallen tree. Ted nervously paced back and forth.

"Kano want a conference with me?" she asked.

"No, it's nothing important."

"You look worry."

"Not worried," he said. "Just curious if you plan on leaving with the others when they go?"

"You are afraid of some ghost?" she joked. "Don't want to be alone on such big island?"

Ted couldn't return her playful energy. He was growing pensive.

"I'm being serious here. What are your plans?"

Lanie shrugged innocently. How could she possibly know that Ted had decided to pursue her? That she was now more important to him than a lifelong dream and he was willing to chuck it all in the hope of spending his life with her, wherever that might be.

"Lanie, what are we?"

She tilted her head, eyes narrowing. "We are… people?"

"No, I don't mean existentially. What's happening between us? Is it serious?"

"Why you asking this, kano?"

"You know why," he sighed. "I can't keep being casual about all this."

"About all what?"

"There's too much at stake now," he said softly. "You know how I feel about you. Have you ever considered… staying here?"

Lanie looked away, grew quiet.

'Tell me you've at least given some thought to what's happening between us."

"Ted, you are rushing."

"I'm not rushing. I just need to know if I can give myself fully to this."

"Kano…"

Her voice was troubled, like she didn't know how to articulate her thoughts.

"You can be honest," he said. "Just tell me. Is this something we should pursue? If you want to travel the world and do your work, I get that. I understand. I wouldn't want to take that from you."

"It's not like that."

"So you'd be willing to stay?"

"Kano, why this important for us to say right now?"

"Because I'm tired of being disappointed."

"How I disappoint you?"

"Not you. It's just the story of my life. Over and over and over."

Lanie looked at her hands, tightened her lips.

"Listen," he said, "I'm sorry if this seems sudden or rushed. I just have to know. Can I give myself to this or not?"

"She's not worth it, kano!"

Ted turned at the sound of a man's voice and saw Philippe plodding toward them, mischief written on his face. "Can't you take the hint?" Philippe said. "She tolerate you so you will let us stay here. Why you think she so nice to you?"

"Philippe!" Lanie shouted.

"It's true!" Philippe answered. "Just tell him! Ted, the reason she nice to you is for our benefit. If she don't show you kindness, you would have put us swimming long time ago. But it's not real. Go find another girl to be your whore."

Lanie and Philippe exchanged sharp words in their language. Ted put his hand in the air to silence the argument.

"Lanie, is that true?" he asked in shock.

"Why you think that way?" she replied, already on the verge of tears.

"Is what he said true? Any of it?"

Lanie sniffled, turned her wet face away from him. Hiding. She fell completely silent.

"Are you being serious right now?" he said in disbelief. "None of it was real? That was all a performance? For what? So I wouldn't kick your friends off the island?"

Philippe spoke in her silence. "Ted, the families got together and asked her to be nice to you. I was there. Go ask Rene. They were all scared after you yell at us. We have nowhere else to go right now. Lanie was the only chance for us to survive here. She became actress for us, but you deserve to know the truth."

Ted's eyes began to glaze, his vision blurred. He peered up at Manny and the other kids splashing around in the distance, his focus going in and out. Lanie looked at the ground and cried as she exchanged quiet, frustrated words with Philippe. She wiped her face with a sleeve and glanced over to Ted, who was still in a daze.

"Ted," she said softly. "I only agree to it in the beginning. Because I care about those children. And you so very angry when you first come to us."

"So then you did agree to this charade? You lied to me?"

"I agreed, kano. But only at first. I don't expect to have feeling for you. But it's not acting for me. Something change."

"How could you?" he groaned.

Lanie turned sharply at Philippe and gave him another earful. Philippe ignored her, turned to Ted. "Kano, she not interested in you. Not then. Not ever. Is time for us to come clean."

Lanie physically shoved Philippe back, continuing to berate him.

Ted raised his voice to bring them to silence. "Stop! Just stop." He took a staggered step back, putting distance between himself and the two strangers in front of him. "I think you should all just stay on this side of the island from this point forward." Ted's eyes then engaged Lanie directly. "*All of you.*"

Ted turned his back to them and stormed away, toward the forest. Lanie shouted after him through her tears, "Kano, I'm sorry. I'm sorry for this!" She switched into her language and continued in a strained whisper, "I'm sorry for everything. Come back. Please."

• • •

As night fell, Ted stood on the wooden dock, ignoring the splinters in his bare feet as he threw his head back and emptied his last bottle of Cabernet Sauvignon. He used the back of his hand to wipe the excess from his chin and then wound up and forcefully launched the bottle far out into the sea. He stumbled slightly as the dark tide rolled in beneath the planks.

Back inside the house, Ted fell onto the couch and started flipping channels. His eyes grew in disgust as two lovers embraced on one of those previously adorable Korean dramas.

Ted yelled at the screen. "Bull. Shit!"

He pulled himself upright and reached for his laptop computer, balancing it on his knees. He launched the writing program and blinked to regain clear vision. Then his fingers went into a flurry of typing.

The betrayal was too much for him. He had loved the girl. But she turned out to be like all the rest. On a whim, he'd dared to dream. But in hoping against hope, he cast his line into the vast waters and caught a nightmare. Humanity had lost its last hero.

Ted struggled to type the last words, and slowly did so before passing out cold where he sat.

The end.

13

NAKO BANGED ON the door a dozen or so times before Ted finally answered, unshaven and wearing his bath robe. The Japanese man sensed that his friend was in a bad way. He peered over Ted's shoulder and saw open luggage on the couch. *Uh oh.*

"Why you not returning my calls, boss?"

Ted sighed and went back to folding and tossing shirts into the suitcase. "I'm sorry, old friend. I can't stay here."

"You going to mainland?"

"Chicago. I'm leaving for good, Nako."

Nako raised an eyebrow, his head jutting forward in disbelief. "You are leaving Island of Ted? What they call it now… Island of Guy Who Live in US?"

"I'm sorry to interrupt our long held tradition of rice ball. But it's something I have to do. It's time."

"Is she going with you?"

Ted froze. Shook his head "no."

Nako saw this one coming. "She hurt you, eh?"

Ted grimaced, bobbed his head. "Not just her. I was actually starting to like them. But what they did was inexcusable. The whole village conspired to make me think I was in love with her."

"Were you?"

Ted dodged Nako's gaze. "It won't happen again."

"Maybe you wrong about her."

"I'm not."

Nako shifted nervously back and forth, hands in his pockets. A quiet moment formed between them. "How about one last game?" Nako asked.

Ted swigged from a beer as they tossed that ragged baseball in a downpour. There was no small talk or shooting the breeze this time. The rain was too loud anyway. Both were soaked but neither cared as they tossed the ball back and forth in what would be their last game.

After this final bonding moment, Ted instructed Nako to come back for him in five days for departure. It was sure to be a daunting journey, and a new chapter in his life, but going back was the only way to quench the loneliness for good. Once Lanie and the others leave the island, things would return to normal, just as they were before he found Manny. But he didn't want to be there when it happened, because even though his anger still boiled toward Lanie, he couldn't easily shake off his feelings for the girl.

Her actions were, in one sense, noble. She wanted only to protect the kids and keep them on the island as long as possible. But in order to accomplish that, she had to put a knife directly through Ted's back—a feeling he knew all too well. He didn't blame her, but it didn't make the hurt any easier to deal with. He had fallen in love with a false persona, being the dope he always was.

But the thought still lingered with Ted… what if it had been real?

14

―――――――――――

BITS OF RAIN began to pelt the island at eleven in the morning. The ground was already mushy from the previous storms, and the angry skies didn't want to relent.

Manny was a quarter mile into the bamboo forest with his older brother, Jorge, and a nine-year-old kid named Nik. They were chasing a lizard with sticks as the svelte prey shot through fallen branches and up a tree. Manny, who was quite fast for his age, led the pack and eventually found himself alone. By the time the other two boys caught up to him, he had stopped dead in his tracks with his head facing downward. The boys circled around him to see a metal box between Manny's feet.

It was black and rusted, with a latch on the side. The top was covered in Japanese writing. Manny stepped away from the box with great care, careful not to trip. Jorge, filled with intrigue, began moving closer to it.

"Wait!" Manny exclaimed in Tagalog.

The boys turned sharply at his voice but Jorge's attention was drawn back to the box.

"I want to see what's inside," Jorge said.

Manny saw a small, rounded steel spike sticking out of the ground. It was just inches from Jorge's foot.

"Don't move, Jorge!" he shouted.

Jorge shrugged and said, "Why not?"

The boy's foot moved and Manny's eyes flew open as his foot came down on the pin. Manny shot toward Jorge with lightning speed and collided with him violently, knocking him back and falling onto the box.

• • •

Ted's entire body jerked forward, spilling hot coffee over the deck railing. At first, he thought it was thunder. And then smoke plumed over the tree line and he knew something was wrong.

He jumped over the rail and dashed for the forest. He ran as fast as his legs would carry him, toward the smoke. He heard a faint commotion far off in the distance.

On the other side of the island, several villagers came out of their tents to see what had happened and then rushed up the embankment.

The wailing of a woman's voice ripped through the air as Lanie and the other villagers made haste toward the smoke. They came to the explosion site and Lanie pushed past a few villagers who stood in stunned silence. The boys were all unconscious. Lanie quickly grabbed Jorge's bloody neck and checked for a pulse. Finding one, she shouted instructions to someone standing nearby and then raced to the younger boy as Jorge slowly opened his eyes.

Ted arrived just as Lanie had spun around toward Manny, who was almost unrecognizable. She paused for a brief moment when the damage began to sink in.

"Dalhin siya sa medical tent now!" she shouted. Ted was also nearing a state of shock as he looked around. He saw fallen trees and smatterings of blood. Ted lifted Manny onto his shoulder while the villagers carried Nik and Jorge. They all rushed toward the south beach village.

Ted entered the medical tent first and laid Manny's limp body onto Lanie's bed. Philippe and Jon followed him in quickly and set the other boys, who were now conscious, flat on the ground. Lanie burst between them and attended to Jorge first. She poured alcohol onto a rag and wiped away a few wounded areas to see the damage. The boy kicked around and convulsed in a state of panic.

"Okay na ang condisyon niya," Lanie said. "Small lacerations only."

Lanie turned to Nik on the floor and doctored his wounds as well, quickly filling a syringe and pumping liquid into the boy's small arm. She dabbed alcohol onto his leg where shards of metal protruded as the boy thrashed wildly, looking around wide-eyed and confused.

Lanie quickly wrapped his bloody leg in a tourniquet and struggled to tighten the rod before it locked into place. She turned to Ted and shouted, "Take here, hold his head!"

Ted immediately took over, elevating the boy's head. Lanie then turned to Manny, who wasn't moving. She hesitated for a moment, not bothering to clean him with alcohol like she had the other boys. She slowly folded her body over his and gave him a motherly hug while checking his pulse with her hand pressed to the side of his butchered neck.

He wasn't breathing. There were no vital signs present.

A tear ran down Lanie's cheek as she filled a syringe and injected it right into his chest. He didn't move or convulse. He just stayed perfectly still. Lanie grabbed a portable defibrillator kit and hit the charge switch. Nothing happened. She smacked the side of the box a few times, bursting the skin on her knuckles. The machine wasn't working. She angrily kicked it away from her.

Lanie swiftly grabbed a small knife and made a vertical incision down his battered chest to his navel. She looked around frantically, searching for something. Ted used his free hand to toss her a box of latex gloves. She quickly removed the gloves and struggled to slide them over her shaking hands. It took an uncomfortable amount of time to get them on. It was hard for Ted to watch.

Lanie cried quietly as she separated Manny's chest cavity with a metal clamp. The villagers looked away in horror as she gently massaged his heart in her hands, trying to force a beat. She massaged over and over and over. Several minutes passed.

Ted's eyes began swelling with tears. Only then did he notice that Manny was missing half of his right arm. Rene put his hand on Lanie's shoulder. She wouldn't stop. He tightened his grip authoritatively and she finally let go. They could all hear Lynette crying outside the tent for her dead son.

Rene gently touched Lanie's face and said, "He's with God now."

Lanie put her bloody hands over her face and cried into them. Along with Rene, the villagers began to latch onto one another as the smallest boy watched the scene unfold with a look of overwhelmed terror on his face.

• • •

The rain stopped falling around nightfall. Lanie sat on the beach watching the tide roll in and out, her medical coat stained red from the blood. Ted watched her from a distance and wondered what to do. He eventually walked over and sat down next to her in the sand. The humid air was thick and salty. They both stared straight ahead and Ted pondered what words of comfort he might use to ease the sting of being overwhelmed with grief. But nothing came to mind. The clouds had momentarily parted, dots of light becoming visible above them. It could have been a perfect night in paradise—in another life. But they'd just lost a fight with reality.

Ted remained beside her, thinking of how she had signed up for exactly this kind of thing. He admired her bravery and now understood just how out of touch he'd been with real life. This is the kind of thing he'd see on the news before flipping channels to something lighter. But this time he was smack in the middle of it, and it placed a heavy strain on his already troubled heart.

Ted grieved for Manny, the small kid whom he'd accosted for taking a few coconuts. He felt like a total bastard.

The villagers took comfort in what the surviving boys had told them.

"Manny fell on the mine to save us," they'd said.

Ted couldn't help but quietly weep as his mind shot back to his first angry encounter with the boy. Ted felt Lanie's body shaking beside him. He moved closer and folded his arm around her. She rested her head on his shoulder as tears fled her tightly closed eyes. He held her for more than an hour like that, neither speaking a word. Neither needing to.

———————————

15

TED STOOD IN the south beach village as rain soaked the entire camp under the glow of moonlight. They encircled the mound of dirt which housed Manny's body. Rene stepped forward and opened his Bible.

"A good name is better than precious ointment, and the day of death than the day of one's birth. It is better to go into the house of mourning, than to go to the house of feasting. For by the sadness of the countenance, the heart is made better. Ecclesiastes, seven."

Ted's eyes found Lanie, whose head was bowed, perhaps in prayer—a grieving soul making petition for the living. She wore her old coat, the one that was torn down the side. Ted figured she must not have been able to wash the blood out of her new one. Lynette sobbed quietly and then fastened onto Rene, who wore a stoic expression of comfort. Ted assumed him to be holding it together in order to strengthen the others. And it worked.

"Today I bury a son," he said, his voice quivering slightly. "But my hope is not in this world but in the paradise to come, when our Lord will make all things new. And there will be no more death or pain, crying or mourning. But for now we suffer these things. I commit Manny's body to the ground in this hope. Goodbye, son."

As the tears streamed down Ted's crimson face, he thought of his own father. Would Pops like what had become of his son? Would he be proud the way Rene was proud of *his* son who had one day earlier given his life to save two others. Ted knew the answer to that question and it was a heavy load to bear.

A feast was thrown that evening in Manny's honor but Ted withdrew to his own side of the island. He entered the massive foyer and looked around at his big screen TV, his leather furniture, the kitchen stocked with his favorite foods. The place he had built suddenly felt cold and lifeless, almost evil. He moved through the mansion like a ghost, picking up and replacing various ornamental items. The word *useless* echoed in his ears and was etched on his face. Finding himself in the spacious kitchen, he grabbed a bottle of aged wine and poured a glass. It wasn't long before he was pouring another.

• • •

Rene found Lanie inside the medical tent tying her hair back with a rubber band. Laughter was heard outside the tent.

Rene looked at her and said, "Will you be joining us? The feast is now starting."

"Hindi, Po. I'm going to see Ted."

"Invite him over. Is good to eat."

Lanie turned to Rene and gave him a hug and a kiss on the cheek before exiting the tent.

A bonfire lit up the beach and fish were cooked over a spit roast. Lanie walked with a heavy sadness, but took a moment to watch the villagers in their moment of healing, before heading into the forest.

• • •

Ted, consumed by alcohol, straddled his couch as loud music blasted from expensive speakers. Not satisfied with the track, Ted stumbled over to the stereo system and began searching through his CDs. Then he heard something. It was familiar, yet strange. *What is that?*

It was the doorbell.

"Why did they install a doorbell?" he thought to himself. Even in a drunken stupor, the irony couldn't escape him. He turned off the radio and heard the bell again.

Good luck telling people I'm not home.

Ted stepped cautiously toward the door. He opened it to find Lanie standing there with a tote bag, looking at him with great concern.

"Sorry to come here," she said. "I know you instruct us to stay on other side. I just want to see if you okay?"

"Wonderful," Ted answered with a slight delay.

Lanie smiled to ease the mood but the look wasn't returned by Ted. He left her standing in the doorway and started walking back to the kitchen. Lanie followed him inside and closed the door behind her.

He began filling another wine glass.

"Would you like a drink?" he asked.

"No, thank you. Ted, I just want to thank you for helping me with the boys."

"Helping?" he sighed. "Yeah."

Ted downed his glass like he was shooting a pill.

"You are drunk? Maybe I come back."

"I might as well be," he said. "It's the only thing to do here in this million dollar palace of shame. Look at this…"

He ran his hand over the counter tops.

"This is Italian marble. My guy out here paid some Filipino workers three dollars a day to install it."

"Ted… what you saying?"

"I'm saying that I'm different. I'm not like you. All I ever wanted was to be alone. To get away from tragedy and death and relationships that only end in disappointment. Now I'm dealing with all same shit! It never ends! There is now officially nowhere else to go."

"Why you say that," she asked. "Ted, can you speak slowly so I can understand?"

He didn't.

"My father died building orphanages in a Mexican slum and I indulge myself in a house so big I get lost going to the bathroom!"

Lanie jumped as Ted smashed his wine glass against the tiled wall of his kitchen.

"And yet here I am... wallowing in pity, spilling my guts to a woman who doesn't understand a word I'm saying."

Lanie searched his eyes, trying to communicate compassion despite the fact that his rapid-fire verbal assault didn't fully compute. Ted stumbled back into the living room.

"Ted, can you please slow down your speaking? I don't understand you so well."

Ted finally obliged, speaking with increased temperance.

"I should not have come here. What was I trying to achieve? How many people have I helped? And you... I don't deserve to have you speak my name out loud."

Ted dropped to his knees, destroyed. Lanie bent down to his level.

"Is reason for you be here. Always a reason."

"Lanie, don't be naïve. You're the one who's here for a reason. This world I've created has done nothing more than make me increasingly aware of how inadequate I am as a human being."

"Is reason for everything, kano."

Ted smirked, almost in tears. He didn't buy that crap for a second.

"Kano," she began in a soft voice. "I think of you in this way… as someone who sacrifice his life for a stranger in the snow. Someone who bring toys to little children. Someone who love and respect his parents. Someone who sees in me only the best things, even after I deceive my special friend. After I failed him."

Lent bent down to his level.

"I wish so bad I could speak in my language, kano, because I want to say something very much… but I don't know it in English."

She sighed in frustration.

Ted fought to steady his eyes on her and said, "Tell me anyway."

Lanie took a moment to consider. Then, suddenly, she began speaking to him in a foreign dialect with great passion and love in her voice. The words came quickly and flowed with emotion. She wept as she spoke, taking breaths between thoughts. Ted was lost in her words, lost in a tidal wave of love. She wiped back tears, with frustration, as her beautiful, unintelligible words spoke directly to his soul. The tenderness and longing in her voice were those of a parent talking to their child for the first time. The rush of words then faded as she found herself unable to take a breath.

Her voice faded away; she was no longer able to speak from the heaviness of her sobbing. A long, palpable silence followed. Lanie reached into her tote bag and removed a shirt that she had made for him. She placed it on the floor beside him and quickly stood up and exited the house.

Ted glanced down at her gift with wet, intoxicated eyes. His fingers grasped the shirt and gently unfolded it.

It was a blue shirt with a white palm tree sewn in the middle. It was too much for him to bear: a gift of love for the unlovable. He took another three shots and passed out.

He slept for twenty-four hours, unable to leave the comfort of his bed. Then, suddenly, he awoke at the sound of wind blowing over his furniture on the deck.

16

LANIE KNELT ON the beach in silent prayer as thunder crackled overhead, her white medical coat flapping in the wind. The villagers were making ropes and tying them to the roofs of their huts. Some were gathering fruit while others patched open windows with banana leaves as the wind grew in intensity.

The locals always knew when something was brewing and were able to distinguish a passing storm from a life-threatening typhoon. This had all the makings of the latter. The camp was bustling with activity, yet Lanie was very still. She knelt lower, with her face almost touching the sand. Rene saw her on the beach and was glad to know that someone had not forgotten to do the obvious.

Meanwhile, Ted sat on the couch with a plate of Pop Tarts, nursing a bad headache. He flipped channels, looking for a weather update since he, unlike the locals, didn't know what to make of the thunder and wind. Finding a news channel, he raised the volume high.

"… expected to hit the southwest Philippine islands in the coming hours. Residents are warned that a level five storm, also known as a Super Typhoon, could possibly emerge, producing winds of 250 kilometers per hour and surges of greater than five meters. Those in the regions of Surigao and Mindanao are urged to take cover immediately."

Ted sat up as his anxiety set in.

"The western edge of the Filipino islands are expected to be the worst hit. Again, travelers are warned that a level five typhoon could strike the Philippines in the coming hours. The storm appears to be picking up steam."

Ted jumped to his feet and stepped onto the deck. The storm that greeted him was a visual spectacle: flashes of lightning revealed palm trees bending, manipulated by fierce winds. Each time the sky lit up, Ted could see an ominous wall of clouds advancing overhead like an unstoppable force. Chills racked his body—he had never seen anything like it before.

Lanie's face entered his mind and suddenly he took no thought of himself; only her, only the girl. Just then, heavy rain began to fall with a boom of thunder, as if someone in the sky had sounded a drum and released the floodgates. Soon Ted had no visibility, even under the strobe of those magnetic lights in the sky. He began to panic.

Reaching for his raincoat and flashlight, Ted blasted out the front door and into the horizontal maelstrom. He ran with all his strength, trusting only in his familiarity with the island as his senses were rendered useless. The fury of the thunder deafened his ears and blankets of rain stopped his vision. Yet he ran.

After taking serious ground, Ted's foot caught a stump and he crashed headlong into the bark of a banana tree, splitting his head open. He stood to his feet in a bloody daze and continued on, picking up even more speed as he cantered through the darkened wetlands.

Swells of rain pounded him without mercy and he despaired that he would ever find the south beach village. Images of Lanie being injured, or worse, assaulted him as he ran. Ted didn't even know what he would do once he got to her, but there was no time for a plan—only action. Suddenly, his foot caught hold once more and he went down hard, this time twisting his ankle. He let out a painful scream but it was stifled by the rain. Ted stood back up and, ignoring the pain, continued his trek toward the south beach area.

After what seemed like an hour, he reached the clearing and sped down the embankment leading to the village with dangerous haste. Rene saw him and immediately ran to greet him.

"Ted… you are bleeding," he shouted, his voice competing with the onslaught of rain.

"It's okay. Are you guys safe? Where's Lanie?"

"She went up to your place."

"What?" Ted said, bewildered. "No."

"She told me she going to your place to see if you okay."

"I came from there… we should've passed each other!"

A boom of thunder caused them both to jump.

"Where is everyone?" Ted asked.

"In their homes. Filipinos know when a storm is coming."

"The news… on the news… it's a typhoon."

Suddenly, they heard the sound of snapping rope. Ted looked over his shoulder and saw the medical tent collapse. He quickly charged over and began digging through the mess, throwing the canvas walls back as he searched deeper.

Ted saw Lanie's Bible on the ground and snatched it up. The pressed flower fell out of its page and the wind blew it away from him. He looked back and saw Rene struggling to nail down a thin beam of wood to reinforce his roof. The rain began to descend with even greater force. Ted fought to move toward Rene as waves began to crash over the beach. It was like moving in quicksand while blindfolded.

Ted grabbed Rene's arm and shouted, "These houses are going to go! The waves will bury this place—it's not safe here! If you stay, everyone will die!"

"There are more than thirty people in this village. What choice we have?"

A look of epiphany hit Ted's face. Suddenly, in that one moment, his entire life made sense.

"My house," he shouted. "They will be safe there. Everyone will fit."

"How far?"

"Just through the forest. Gather your family and I'll go and tell the others!"

Another wave crashed onto the island. The situation was becoming desperate. Ted raced from house to house, instructing them in broken English to get up and follow him.

Forty villagers—men, women and children—trekked through the mud as the trees swayed and bent violently. The villagers could hear the sound of snapping branches, above the rain, as their senses were assaulted from every angle. Flashes of lightning allowed them to move forward with some bearings. The wind was fierce, howling with anger as the villagers fought tooth and nail for every step.

Ted led the pack, with Jorge snug in his arms. He grunted and battled as the forward march progressed. He had already forgotten about his head being split open and the twisted ankle: this was life or death. His eyes searched for Lanie each time the relentless lightning lit up the forest. He saw no trace of her.

Suddenly, one of the boys lost his footing and sailed backward. Rene's hand caught the boy's arm and pulled him in close. The wind continued to blow like a freight train as crashing waves could be heard from the beach. Just then, they saw a pinpoint of light in the distance: Ted's porch light.

It became a beacon of hope, of safety. The villagers trudged on, making slow, but steady, progress toward the light. The rice stalks under their feet were flat against the earth, having given up the fight. Still, the surge of humanity went forward with Ted at the helm.

And yet, he did not find Lanie.

17

TED REACHED THE porch first and flung the door open to let the villagers enter, one by one. He felt like Noah gathering people into his ark. The house was serene inside, a huge contrast from the fury that raged outside. Ted noticed, as the last person entered, that the villagers were all looking around in amazement. It occurred to him that these people had probably never seen a place as spectacular as this mansion, which he had considered to be a monument to his failure as a man—as a son. But things seemed very different at that moment.

He ran through the house, looking for any sign of Lanie. Rene found him in the bedroom, looking ill from worry. He dropped Lanie's Bible onto his bed and sat down with his face in his hands. He looked up and saw the wind and rain pounding against the deck outside.

"I need to find her, Rene."

"I will go. You stay here."

"No," Ted demanded. "Stay and take care of your family. I can do it."

Rene looked into Ted's eyes and saw that there would be no bargaining with him. "We'll be in prayer for you until your return."

Ted put his hand against Rene's shoulder—a gesture of gratitude—then hurriedly made for the door.

Once outside, Ted sensed that he had leaped into harm's way. His head turned back, very briefly, and saw the villagers through the window. They were all inside, and safe.

Ted quickly surveyed the land as palm leaves and pieces of bark snapped and whistled past his head. He ran into the rice field and over the terraces. The lightning was constant, allowing him to see despite the driving rain. He fought forward with every ounce of strength in his body. His eyes burned, his ankle in torturous pain. Ted was determined not to fail.

"Lanie!" he shouted.

He ran like someone under water. The scene in front of him was a dreamlike maze of debris and downpour. Snapping branches echoed the violence of the story around him.

"Lanie!" he yelled until his lungs hurt.

His shouts sounded like whispers against the typhoon. He screamed for the girl with all his might and soul, the veins in his neck standing taut against the skin.

Thunder boomed and felt like it shook the island. Ted staggered through the forest on wobbly legs, knowing Lanie was not on the path.

"I would have seen her," he thought.

Just then, a faint voice resonated in his ears. He looked in all directions, waiting for the lightning to give him sight. He heard it again—just a whisper.

Another boom!

Ted focused his eyes in the direction of the sound, waiting for a flash of lightning.

A single crackle, met with a flash, gave him a vision that would be burned in his mind forever. He saw her in the distance, fighting to move toward him. He saw her mouth open, screaming his name in silence. He ran for her.

They moved toward one another in flashes of light until he grabbed her hand and pulled her in. A coconut shot through the forest on a gust of wind and Ted moved her out of the way just as the coconut smashed against a tree with the force of a speeding bullet. Ted led her by the arm as they made their way back toward the house.

Rene was kneeling with a few others in a semicircle when the door opened. They all turned with some measure of anticipation and saw Ted and Lanie, drenched and bloody, enter the living room. The villagers jumped to their feet and ran to them, greeting them with profound joy. A loud applause erupted! Ted looked around the large room, with Lanie by his side, and saw that all of the villagers were safe. Philippe stood in the corner, locking eyes with Ted. Not a word was spoken, but Ted saw unflinching gratitude on the man's face. It was enough.

Ted led Lanie upstairs into the loft and turned to face her, both of them looking worse for wear.

"What happened to you?" he asked.

"I go to see if you're safe. We can see a storm is coming."

"I'm so glad you're okay," he said. "I don't know what I would've done if…"

She put her finger to her lips to quiet him.

"We not so different, kano."

They both looked over the second-floor railing and saw the entire south beach village engaging in a prayer of thanks. Ted was moved as they thanked God for protecting him. He looked into her eyes and she winked.

"Is reason for you be here, kano."

Ted let that sink in for a moment before conceding. "I know."

The storm beat against Ted's house for nine hours with tremendous force, but not even a single window was broken. Wind and wave attacked the mansion but it stood under the pressure. Ted's mind was drawn back to the first time he'd laid eyes on the place and Nako had told him, "The roof is reinforced with a special oak for rainy season. You'll need that."

Ted could only smile.

As the fog lifted, a weary drizzle fell on the mushy ground where the south beach village once stood. There wasn't a house or tent in sight—nothing but broken wood, leaves, and large puddles of water. The ocean was at peace; a village, gone.

Part Three

"He who is not every day conquering some fear has not learned the secret of life."

-Ralph Waldo Emerson

ONE

I WOKE UP to a house full of chatter. Peering up through the blanket, it took a moment to understand what was going on.

Oh, yes, I remembered. New housemates.

Lanie and the kids slept on a pallet on my bedroom floor. Before you judge, I offered valiantly to take the floor instead, but Lanie would not hear of it. She said a man must sleep in his own bed. She was soft-hearted but hard-headed.

I freshened up a bit and then introduced the smaller kids to Pop Tarts, although they preferred drinking coconut water. Weirdoes.

Rene cooked up a big batch of adobo, which is a salty dish of sautéed dark-meat chicken in a bath of vinegar and soy sauce. With forty people living downstairs, the man had his work cut out for him.

After lunch I found Lanie alone on the bamboo deck. Not wanting to disturb someone in deep thought, I was relieved when she turned to me and smiled. Seeing her brought up many memories; some pleasant, others painful. It had been a few days since the typhoon hit and I had had ample time to think about my situation. It seemed something was drawing me away. I no longer felt like a loner in the world. The south beach villagers were my friends and I genuinely liked all of them. When Manny died I felt like I had lost my own son, prompting a level of guilt which led to a bout of alcohol poisoning. I loved them. But I had a painful decision to make, the most painful of my life.

Lanie's hair smelled like coconut and lavender as I sat down next to her and gazed at the lagoon.

"I want to thank you for what you did," she said. "You save us."

"Listen," I said, clumsy as ever. "I just…"

Her eyes narrowed, teasing me.

"What's matter, cat has eaten your tongue?"

I smiled and said, "This is hard."

"What—are you courting another girl?" she said, grinning to ease my nerves.

"Have dinner with me tonight."

"Someone is asking a date?" she said.

"Yes. A date."

She offered a quiet, nervous laugh and said, "I accept, kano."

• • •

Nako steered the boat over peaceful waters. Below deck I sat on a rice bag in an undersized suit. Hey, in a place like this you get what you can get. Lanie sat across from me in a black evening gown. We looked so out of place on this dirty boat and I had a hard time not staring at her. I could tell she had no idea how amazing she looked. And how strange, I thought, that she'd ever taken the slightest interest in me. Maybe it was even real at times.

She shouted to me over the noise of the motor. "Where we going to again?"

"It's a surprise. You look nice, by the way. I wasn't sure if Nako knew what I meant by *ladies' evening wear.*"

Lanie struggled with a stringy shoulder strap, as if she wasn't used to formal clothes. I looked up and saw Nako on the bow drinking noodles and steering with his free hand. He shot me a wink.

I'd planned this date with great care but it was a sad moment for me. This would be the end of our courtship and I knew I wouldn't see Lanie again after tonight. That's why I wanted this evening to happen: at least once we'd get to be two people in formal clothes, having a grown-up moment.

Looking at her across the boat, my heart broke. She gave me a cute grin, not having a clue that it would be our last night. I'm sure in her mind this was the beginning and not the end, but it wasn't for us. I loved her. Deeply. But I knew that her calling was here, helping the needy and making children smile. I wished so badly that I could be a man worthy of her, but it seemed selfish of me to pretend that I was.

The truth is, I hadn't changed much. I was still the same guy I was when I first set foot on the island, except for a new appreciation for the human race. But other than that, I was the same Ted who wanted everything his way and was still more comfortable around Hollywood people than the genuine folks I'd met here. At least in the movie business I could feel morally superior at times. But not here. Not around these people. Not around Lanie.

A chunk of my heart lay in the Philippines and much of it belonged to the girl sitting across from me, struggling to get comfortable in that dress.

• • •

As the sun faded into the horizon, we stepped off the boat and I offered Lanie my hand. She staggered a bit to master her high heels and gave me an embarrassed grin.

We sat across from one another in a five-star restaurant overlooking the water. This part of the islands hadn't seen much damage, so it was business as usual. I scanned the menu, recognizing nary a thing on it.

"Oh, this sounds good. What is balut?"

"It's duck egg with baby duck on the inside."

Okay—moving on. I turned to the waiter.

"I'll have a steak. Medium rare. Mixed greens on the side."

Lanie smiled and said, "That's okay for me too."

The waiter nodded and went on his way, leaving us with two glasses of pinot noir.

"Kano, why you bring me this nice place?"

"Just a token of friendship."

Lanie began to dab at her eye but I just figured she wasn't accustomed to wearing makeup. Then I noticed tears.

"Hey, don't do that," I said softly. "What's wrong?"

"I don't like goodbye," she said.

She was more perceptive than I thought. "How did you know?"

"In your face. I can see."

I handed her my handkerchief.

"Listen," I said. "Please… don't be sad. This is the best thing. I know it doesn't make sense now but this is something I have to do. I turned over the house to Rene and the others. It's the only good thing I've ever done in my life."

She paused while dabbing her eyes. "If that will make you happy."

Watching her cry was hard. She then smiled unexpectedly and looked at me with warmth. "Ted, can I ask?"

"Of course."

"Why did you find interest in me?"

I fiddled with my silverware, thinking of how silly it was that she thought to ask. Anyone with eyes and ears would take an interest in her. So I bluffed.

"It's your money."

She laughed and threw the handkerchief at me. But I knew she deserved a real answer so I racked my brain, thinking of a way to articulate those initial feelings that had come on so strong.

"I think I know the reason," I began. "This baffles me, but you are somehow able to look past everyone's faults. Even this idiot kano who says all the wrong things." I took a breath, wondering how much truth I should be sharing. "It's like you see a version of me that doesn't really exist."

"Like what? How?"

"Like the way you're looking at me right now. Even in my darkest moment you told me I had a purpose on that island, and I didn't believe you."

"You should learn to listen to me."

I felt like she was making an appeal, and it crushed me.

"If I had more time." It's all I could say.

She immediately stood, crossed over to me and gave me a tight hug. It was quick. Then she was back in her seat.

"I will miss you, kano."

"They need you, Dr. Lanie. The Island of Ted needs you. And take my bedroom. I insist on it."

"I prefer the sitting chair," she said. "Suits me better."

Lanie folded her napkin and placed it in her lap, then sat up straight and smiled through watery eyes.

"You will write to me," she said, not asking. "A lot."

"Of course I will. You're my girl." My face felt warm as I took in her reaction. "Always will be."

Lanie and I waited outside the restaurant while Nako went to fetch a taxi. We tried not to look at one another.

"I hope your flight is safe," she said.

"It's the ferry I'm worried about."

"Ferry is so fun. It's adventure, kano."

Nako pulled around with the taxi driver and waved us over.

Standing still, I told her, "Nako's going to take you back. I didn't want to draw this out too long. You understand."

She nodded *yes*.

I touched her shoulders and said, "My mind is saying goodbye but my mouth can't seem to say it."

Lanie touched my lips and said it for me, her soft voice a tremble. "Goodbye."

And with that, she crossed the street, got into the taxi and drove away. I stood frozen, for what seemed like ten minutes, with my hand in the air, waving at the car as it got smaller and smaller in the distance. It was the hardest moment of my entire life.

TWO

LOS ANGELES LOOKED like an alien planet as I stepped off the plane. Thirteen hours of sleep in a posh downtown hotel couldn't even clean out the cobwebs. It wasn't all bad news though: I needed a job and Roger Graham had one waiting. His alien movie was in post production and Roger had already set up meetings for me to supervise the edit and get things locked up and ready for a summer release. I sat through a three-hour cut of the film and almost lost my mind. It was tedious, to say the least.

Everything here in the States felt like it was moving at warp speed and my phone never stopped buzzing. I was constantly on the run, checking my e-mail and text messages, in and out of meetings—I was already worn out after just two weeks back on the job.

One such meeting brought me to an upscale Greek restaurant, where I was to meet with a market analyst. However, I very quickly found out that Roger had called this meeting just to set me up with someone—his way of saying, "Welcome back." I sat at the table, uncomfortable and bored, as the conversation wore on.

"Ted, it's like so cool that you went overseas to visit those poor people," my chipper twenty-five year-old date said with a faux LA accent. "Roger told me all about it."

"Yeah. It was actually…"

"Totally. Hang on for two secs."

The girl then giggled as she read something on her iPhone and decided to type out a lengthy response as I looked around the room.

"You writing a book over there?" I joked.

"Nah, just my girl, Jen. We were supposed to hang tonight but I think she got an STD from some New Jersey douche with a tacky tongue bolt. She like wanted me to meet up with his boy later but I was like… you freak! I'm not hooking up with some house-painter who thinks he's an actor. What a loser!"

"Listen, I'm not sure what Roger told you, but I'm not looking to get into a relationship with anyone. I just got back into town and…"

"No probs. If you just want to party, I'm down with that. Hey, do you know if they are casting for the new Toby Maguire flick yet?"

The girl then turned her attention to some chipped paint on her nail and almost fell into hysterics.

"Dude, that is like the last friggin' time I let one of those chinks touch my nails. And to think… they're supposed to be like the best at manicures! Those bitches have *totally* ruined my day!"

It probably took her five minutes to realize I'd thrown down a few bills and walked out of the restaurant.

I spent that evening in a luxury suite at the Hilton that Roger had booked for me until I found a more permanent place to settle. Sleep was difficult. I wondered what Lanie was doing.

Was she wearing that white doctor's coat out of habit, even inside the house where there were no mosquitoes? Was she wearing her hair down or in a ponytail? Did she find the box under my bed that I'd left there by mistake? Was she lonely at night or did the kids keep her occupied?

Those thoughts swirled in my head, as did other questions, like, "What would Pops say right now?" and "Would he be proud of me?"

I never knew how to answer that last one. In fact, it was a strange question to ask myself because there never was a time, in all my memories, in which Pops acted like he was disappointed in me. Bewildered, yes, but not disappointed. So where was this coming from? I simply didn't know the answer to that.

In the evenings I worked on my screenplay, which I hoped to finish in the next few weeks and hand to Roger at just the right time. It was the kind of film I should have made early on in my career—commercial appeal, yet full of heart and realism.

And yes, I had changed the ending.

THREE

IT WAS A quarter past four when I rolled into the theater room to watch the trimmed-down, two-hour-and-forty-minute cut of the film. The edit was smoother, but something still bothered me and I couldn't put my finger on it. The pacing seemed fine, the acting decent—for this genre—and the action beats were well timed. Still, it felt like there was a missing piece. And then, in a moment of epiphany, it came to me.

"It's the script," I said aloud.

The other executives who were sitting with the editor turned to me.

"Sorry, Ted?"

"I said it's the script. The story is what's flawed here. Our hero ends up with the wrong woman."

"This is what the audience wants to see... we've tested this part of the film and everyone agrees it's the right move."

"I don't see it though, Fred. It's obvious he's in love with the Star Queen's maidservant so I don't buy the ending. Why does he choose the Queen instead?"

"Uh…" the executive stammered, expecting the answer to be obvious. "Because the Star Queen is Angelina Jolie."

I was surprised to see Roger standing in the doorway, gently gesturing for me to come over. As I approached, he took my arm and said, "Walk with me, Teddy."

We ended up at a café down the block where Roger complained about his food to a waitress in such a caustic tone that she actually began to fear for her job. I did manage to calm him down with a bit of effort.

Between bites, he told me, "These schmucks, they don't know story. They know action, they know delivery… but they don't know story. I'm with you on that. Your instincts are still good."

"It still feels too long. Maybe we have them cut it down to two fifteen?"

"Hey!" Roger barked at the waitress again.

He pointed to his half-full glass of iced tea with his chubby finger and raised an eyebrow.

"You want me to get my own drinks from now on? Maybe I'll go ahead and tip myself while I'm at it, sweetheart."

"I'm sorry, sir," she responded before filling his glass so nervously that she overfilled, causing some of the tea to run down the sides.

"Why don't you just get lost before you screw up my lunch even worse. Go ahead—scram."

Roger Graham, ladies and gentlemen.

Somehow, at that moment, my mind traveled back to Delores and the Christmas tree, sitting with her and her kids, drinking tap water and laughing at one another.

As my thoughts returned to the current conversation, Roger was in the middle of some rant about poor service and "the good old days."

Over the next few weeks I began to seclude myself in the suite. The edit was rolling along well enough without me and I was beginning to feel that loneliness which plagued me eighteen months earlier, before I bought an island and fell in love with a girl. I looked around my 2,000-square-foot hotel room and wondered how cool it would've been to show it to Manny and let him run around and play.

I was constantly surrounded by people and, yet, I felt extremely hollow inside. Did I make the right choice with Lanie? Of course I did. She belonged in the company of better souls. But for some reason, time wasn't healing that wound yet.

I watched another re-run of Jimmy Fallon and channel surfed for a while before landing on a guy in a suit talking to me in a deep voice.

"Coming up next on Turner Classics: Richard Goldstone's 1962 classic, *No Man Is An Island*."

I tilted my head toward the ceiling, toward a God who must have timed that one perfectly. "Funny," I told him aloud.

Another two months passed and I had finished my screenplay. I gave it to Roger on a Wednesday and we met at Graham Entertainment to discuss the project that Friday. He called me into his cigar-lounge of an office and I took a seat in front of his huge desk. His chair was always elevated so he could literally look down his nose at people during a meeting. He was smiling though, and that's a good sign.

"So what did you think?" I launched right in.

"I won't lie to you, Teddy. You know I always shoot from the hip."

Uh oh.

"The script, it's sorta, well… how do I say this. It's horse shit."

"Beg your pardon?" I said, trying to swallow.

"It's awful, Ted. Where's the action?"

"It's not that kind of story. I went in a different direction with it. It's a love story."

"There's nothing believable about your plot. Ted, when you popped up in LA five months ago I thought my right hand man was back. But this…" he said, pointing to my script. "This is not the Ted I mentored. This is… corny."

I looked away, hurt.

"Look," he said. "Don't be like that. You had to know this script was crap. I mean, the female character, what's her name… Lanie. I just don't buy it. Nobody talks that way in the real world… she's a complete phony."

"Roger," I interrupted.

He looked startled. I don't think anyone had ever cut him off mid-tirade before.

"Um… yeah?"

"Don't say that name."

"What name?"

"The one you just said. I'd rather you not say that name again."

"What, Lanie? It's your character, not mine."

"Just don't say that name, okay?" My voice was loud and forceful. "When you say it… it sounds profane."

"What the hell is wrong with you?"

His eyes were growling at me. And I didn't care.

"Just don't say that name out loud. Not in front of me. Not ever."

"Excuse me, where do you even get off…"

"I have to go," I interrupted once more.

I stood up and walked toward the door. Then I heard him call after me.

"Ted!"

I turned to face him.

"What happened to you over there?" he asked. "I've been meaning to talk to you about this but… you are not yourself anymore."

"Good," I declared. "Maybe I'm healed."

FOUR

———————————

FROM THAT MOMENT on, I knew exactly what I wanted. And, more importantly, I also knew that I could, or would, be the man she needed and deserved. No longer did I see myself the way Roger and Teresa saw me. Now I was beginning to see myself the way Lanie saw me. And that was good news.

Pops had once said, "Love is forgetting faults and remembering only the good."

It was strange how much influence my late father's words were having on my life. It was almost as if he knew the battles I was going to fight in life and that he, for whatever reason, knew that he wasn't going to be there to fight alongside me. I'm sure Pops had his faults too, but I never knew him to tell a lie, or even to exaggerate a tale in order to get my attention. He was an entirely decent man. And I was seeing more and more of him in me every day.

Maybe that's what Lanie saw too, only she saw it first. Relationships had always been difficult for me, but now I knew one thing for sure: I was meant to live out my days on that island, with the people I loved. And with her.

• • •

I had closed all of my credit cards the first time I left for the island, leaving only a bank and savings account open. I headed to the bank early in the morning because I didn't want to wait. I was even more anxious to leave the States this time because what awaited me was no longer a mystery, but a destiny. I told the bank manager I'd once more be traveling overseas and that any foreign charges to my account were completely normal, and that a freeze should not be placed on my funds for any reason whatsoever. They temporarily halted any fraud protection for Japan and the Philippines, my only two stops.

Knowing my flight would be leaving at ten o'clock sharp the following day, I headed to the mall to pick up some new clothes—hoping to further impress the girl—and to grab a few gifts for Rene and his family. I also found a cute wooden sailboat and some new baseball mitts that I picked up for Nako.

After so many months away, I really missed my friends. I also perused some diamond engagement rings but remembered how Lanie had once told me she thought expensive rings were such a waste. The way she put it was more like, "Girls with big diamond work on red lights in Manila." That was her way of calling them whores, I think. No—she was a simple girl who desired simple things. A big engagement ring might actually offer an unintended offense.

It's so hard to adapt to another culture's way of seeing things, especially if said cultures share only the faintest of commonalities.

• • •

It was 72 degrees in LA when I boarded a Delta flight to Narita-Tokyo. There I'd have a four-hour layover before heading to Manila. Then it would be just like last time: cab ride to the nearest hotel to sleep off the jetlag, then wake up and catch another flight to Cebu City, an eight-hour jeep ride to a ferryboat, which, a day later, would put me at the docks of Surigao.

From there I'd meet up with Nako and an hour later, I'd be on the Island of Ted. I had already taken the trip once, and another time in reverse, so I knew it would be painful. But not nearly as painful as leaving. On the flight back to LA I couldn't get an image out of my mind—it was Lanie's face, wet with tears, the last time I saw her on the street outside the restaurant. Talk about breaking a guy's heart, I thought I was going to die right there in my seat on a dodgy airplane. But once I got to LA everything was so hectic and distracting that it was easier to forget about her.

This time it was different because I wasn't running from love, but toward it. So I didn't mind the grueling travel one bit. I had called Nako earlier in the week and relayed my itinerary, but warned him not to tell Rene or the others. I wanted to surprise them. Nako's voice was excited on the phone and when he talks fast he breaks into spontaneous Japanese and totally loses me. But I got the gist of his sentiment—*he missed me too.*

The flight seemed longer than usual because I couldn't sleep a wink. I was too excited to sleep, thinking only that I'd be back on the island in three short days. I felt like a kid the night before Christmas, waiting to open all of his presents on what was always the longest night of the entire year!

After a great many hours and a severely cramping back, we crested over Tokyo and I felt a mix of emotions as we hit the tarmac at Narita Airport. I was almost home.

FIVE

NIGHT HAD FALLEN when I boarded the plane to Manila. I felt uneasy for some reason. My life had been one big irony after another so dying in a plane crash when I was so close to seeing Lanie again gave me pause. A rush of energy hit my tired body when we took off and immediately encountered turbulence.

"No turning back now," I thought.

The next two hours would find me twice puking in the air-toilet from nervousness. I tried to watch a stupid movie, which our studio had produced, on the plane's shared jumbo screen. I then felt like puking for a different reason.

The plane's metallic hiss kept me on edge until the captain came over the radio and announced that we were making our final descent into Manila. The approach was slow, taking twenty or so minutes. I could've crawled right out of my skin from the mounting anxiety and tension. Then, finally, we landed. I stepped off the plane and into the tunnel at Ninoy-Aquino and felt a massive, invisible hug forming around me. The place felt familiar and warm.

"Almost there," I thought… again.

I'd anticipated standing in line for hours, but it didn't matter; I was grounded, at least. After getting a passport stamp and grabbing my luggage, I looked around for a place to exchange money, something I forgot to do my first time here. All of the counters had long lines and my leg muscles were beyond shredded. Then I spotted a bare kiosk with no line and headed over to exchange five hundred dollars for Filipino Pesos. I took my wad of cash, stuffed it in my shorts and headed out for a taxi, familiar with the routine.

Coming out of the airport terminal, I was hit with a blast of Filipino aroma—the sweet smell of gasoline and barbecue smoke to welcome me home. This time it made me hungry. I asked the taxi driver, in broken Tagalog, if we could pull over for a bite to eat. I told him he could join me and I'd pay for his food.

He surprised me by pulling his car onto the sidewalk to park.

"Oh yeah, they do that here," I remembered.

We ducked inside a busy food shack and despite being two in the morning, I was already sweating from the heat pouring out of the kitchen. The air outside was also more humid than I'd remembered. We ate a plate of pancit and lumpia and the driver drank a couple of beers. About that time I decided to check for any missed calls from Nako and dug around in my pocket for my cell phone. But it wasn't there.

I stood up, frantic. My hands searched all over my body, looking for the phone. I got up and ran back to the taxi, looking for it everywhere. Then I re-traced my steps into the restaurant, but there were far too many people standing around. I asked a teenager if he'd seen a phone on the ground and he blew cigarette smoke into my face as his friends laughed.

I went back inside the restaurant and the cabbie walked over, looking concerned.

"Is there some problem?" he asked.

"Yeah—I think I lost my phone. I need it to make the rest of my travel plans."

"Well, if you don't find it, they have phone at the hotel you can use."

"I know, but it had all my contact numbers in it."

He shrugged and the waitress handed me a tab. Our total came to 264 pesos. That's around $6 US, a day's wage over here. I counted out the money and handed it to her. She looked at the money with a strange expression, and then handed it back to me.

"No, you can keep the change. It's all right."

She shook her head "no."

The cabbie grabbed the bills and inspected them for all of two seconds.

"This fake pesos."

"What do you mean?" I said, snatching the bills.

The waitress then handed me the correct bills from her fanny pack for comparison. Mine were definitely fake bills. I turned to look at the cabbie and his expression was grave.

"I'm sorry, I… this is all I have. Is there a place to exchange money around here?"

"Only at the airport," he said, while opening his wallet and handing the waitress some money. I felt terrible.

"No, you don't have to pay—I'll go find someone to exchange with me!" I shouted over the noise of the room.

I ran outside and bumped into some teenage girls, who gave me the once-over and rolled their eyes. The street was unfamiliar and packed with nightlife. I had no idea where to go, so I stepped into the street, looking for a MoneyGram or Western Union sign. There were none. I then heard the taxi's engine and I turned around. The cabbie was leaving. I rushed over to his car and he glanced up at me, peeved.

"Listen, I'm sorry… I didn't know they were fake. Just take me to an exchange center and I'll pay you back for the food and for the ride."

I tried to remember some Tagalog in my frantic state and said, "Magbabayad ka! Bayad ako!"

He sighed, looked down, and then reluctantly signaled for me to hop back in.

We drove a few blocks and he spotted a 24-hour exchange. I exited the cab, apologizing all the while, and rushed inside. After five minutes of waiting in line I put down my bank card and said, "I need to exchange five hundred US dollars."

The lady behind the glass partition took my card and swiped it through her machine. Her eyes narrowed a bit and she swiped it again. And again.

She handed the card back to me and said, "I'm sorry, sir, but do you have another card?"

"Another card?" I said, getting angry. "This is my personal debit card from the US—I should be able to use it. It wasn't a problem the last time I was here."

She took my card again and swiped it. Then nodded.

"I'm sorry, sir—there is a problem with your bank. You will need to contact them."

"Do you have a phone?"

"No, sir. But there's a pay phone you can use in hotels. Do you need a directory?"

"No," I said. "I don't have money to use a pay phone. That's what I'm trying to get right now. I need to exchange money."

"I'm sorry, sir but we don't have a phone for international calling."

"Well…. can you just tell me what the problem is? What does your screen say?"

She looked at the monitor and said, "Says here there is fraud alert on your card."

"Dammit!" I yelled. "I told them I'd be traveling overseas! I hate banks!"

She just looked at me.

"I'm sorry, sir. Can you please resolve with your bank and step aside for the next person?"

Her voice wasn't mean. She just had no way of dealing with a frantic American in her limited English. I stepped outside and saw the cabbie leaning on his hood, smoking a cigarette. He looked up at me and I shrugged.

"I'm sorry," was all I could say.

He nodded, almost like he expected as much, and opened the trunk so I could take my luggage.

"Someone stole my phone and my bank cut off my funds. I didn't mean to waste your time, sir."

I took off my watch and offered it to him. He took the watch and gave me a pat on the shoulder.

"It's worth six hundred dollars," I said.

He got back inside the car and pulled away as I stood with five bags of luggage on some unknown street in downtown Manila at three in the morning. Things were not looking good for my survival.

SIX

———————————

A COUPLE OF kids rushed over to grab my bags, hoping they were going to get a tip. They looked like good kids, too, and reminded me of Manny. I felt terrible telling them "no" but I had nothing on me except for some counterfeit bills that would probably get them thrown into jail. My eyes were heavy; I'd been awake for a very long time. So I loaded up my bags, using every appendage like a coat rack, and began walking. After a few blocks I found a concrete building carved out of an alleyway—that looked like some kind of hotel—and headed in that direction. I waddled through the door, catching it hard against my shoulder as it sprang back, and then dropped all of my luggage in the lobby. The thud probably woke up half the guests.

There was a dilapidated wooden desk with a flower pot on it. Below my feet was chipped hardwood and there was a mirror at the far end of the room, from which I caught my reflection. My hair was a mess, I was drenched in sweat, and my clothes were twisted in every possible direction.

A man in a yellow, collared shirt stepped out of a back room and smiled at me.

"Hello, sir. How many guest?"

I approached the desk, trying to remember how those Hollywood actors could create sympathy with just a look. I tried to mimic that look.

"I'm sorry to bother you but I lost my cell phone and I need to call my bank."

"Is it local bank?"

"No," I admitted. "It's in the States."

"I see. You can dial out and we charge the call to your room."

I wasn't sure how that was going to work out, but I gave it a shot. Of course, the number brought me to a menu of options, so I held 0. After twenty minutes of waiting, I heard a voice.

"Hello, and thank you for calling…"

"I need help!" I said in a panic. "You guys cut off my account and I told you I was going overseas. Can you please…"

"I'm sorry, sir—can you slow down? Did you say there was a fraud alert on your card?"

"Yes, but this call is costing me fifteen dollars a minute so you'll excuse the rush. My name is Ted LaSalle and I need you to unfreeze my account."

"Okay, sir—let me transfer you over to our fraud alert department."

"Wait!" I exclaimed. "Don't put me on…"

And I was once again on hold. This time they left me on hold for twenty-five minutes before I heard the sound of doom—a muted click followed by a dead dial tone.

"Would you like to call again?" the man asked me in a worried tone.

"I'm so sorry but I can't afford another call. In fact, I can't afford *that* call."

"Do you live close to here?" he asked.

I drew in a long breath and said, "I live off the coast of Surigao."

"That's… very far from here," he nodded.

"I just need some help. Is there any way you can help me?"

There was a long pause and the man looked around, then suspiciously wrote something down in a register book. He quickly handed me a key.

"Go up stairs," he said in a low voice. "Stay in room thirteen. If goes past noon I will have to charge you."

I felt like reaching over the counter and giving him a big hug. I grabbed my bags and headed up a short staircase to a landing. The hallway led me to room thirteen and I stepped inside a tired, but thankful, man. I lay down without changing clothes and fell into a deep, coma-like sleep. I dreamed about Lanie.

We were in a dark room with no doors and couldn't find our way out. I began kicking the walls as hard as I could until a pinpoint of light shone on the wall nearest her. She placed her hand on my shoulder and I became calm instantly. I reached out and put my fingers into the light and it slowly enveloped my whole body. At once I was free but I looked back through the tiny pinhole and saw Lanie still in the dark room with no doors. She was calling out for me but I couldn't get to her. There was no way to get back inside. Then the pinhole closed and I lost sight of her.

I snapped awake, sweating and disoriented. Sitting up, I saw the bedside clock was showing 11:15. I'd missed my local flight to Cebu.

I took a quick shower and changed clothes before heading into the street with all of my luggage, thanking the clerk with a head-nod on my way out. I immediately flagged down a taxi and he pulled to the curb, got out and walked over to place my bags in the trunk.

I quickly stopped him and said, "Can you take me to the US embassy?"

He shook his head *no*. "Embassy closed for national holiday."

I realized that it was also Friday here in the Philippines, which meant that the embassy would not re-open until Monday. I was now convinced that I would be sleeping on the streets for the next three nights. I was also convinced that I may not survive these streets.

The cabbie said, "Sorry," and headed back to the driver's side.

"Wait!" I hollered, thinking fast. "Can we make a deal?"

"Ano?" he said.

"Magpalatin," I told him, trying to remember the right term. "Me and you... kalakalan."

"You want a trade?"

"Yes!" I exclaimed. "Can you drive me? I need to get to Surigao."

"You need boat to Surigao."

"I know that. But I missed my flight and don't have a phone to..." It was clear I was losing his interest. "I just need some help."

I then noticed him eyeballing my luggage.

"There's some boats leaving that way. But the loading dock is far."

"I'll give you two suitcases, including what's inside, for bayad."

He took a long moment, flipped a cigarette into his mouth and then unzipped the bags, picking the two that were filled with my newly purchased clothing.

"You give me these two?"

"Fine," I sighed, running out of options.

"You don't have money—how you gonna pay for ferry?"

I shrugged, looking down at my remaining bags. He smiled and put my luggage into the trunk. I hopped onto the front seat of the cab and we were off. The temperature was rising into the upper 90s and my cabbie refused to turn on the air conditioner. To make matters worse, my window was jammed and wouldn't roll down, so the long ride to the docks felt like being stuck in a sauna.

I had no money for water and the cabbie was apparently used to long treks in the heat. To keep my spirits up my thoughts returned to Lanie and how great it was going to feel to see her again. I just wished it could happen sooner.

A couple of miles from the docks, the cabbie pulled onto the gravel shoulder; we had a flat tire. He jumped out, removed his shirt, and retrieved a spare tire from his trunk. It began to dawn on me that, in light of these recent events, God might not want me to make it back to the island. It was only a passing thought, but one that scared me terribly.

Twenty minutes later we arrived at the docks and I thanked the cabbie and bid him farewell. He happily drove away with two thousand dollars' worth of clothes, the only apparel I had left. As always, the docks were bustling with activity, so I searched for a friendly face or anyone with a captain's hat. Finding the latter, I rushed over with my remaining bags.

"Are you going to Surigao?"

He looked at the sweaty, panicked American in front of him and shook his head. He then pointed to the ticket booth.

"No, I need to find a vessel. No ticket."

He just stared at me so I lugged my bags to the next official-looking guy I saw.

"Excuse me… I'm trying to get to Surigao City. Do you have any boats heading that way?"

He nodded, smiling.

"Yes, sir. Show your ticket to the man standing behind the ropes and he get you on."

"I don't have a ticket. I only have these bags."

He looked at my remaining luggage.

"Can we make a deal—the two of us?"

He looked around suspiciously like the guy at the hotel had done, then nodded and grabbed my bags and instructed me to step over the rope. He then personally escorted me onto the bow of the ship and said he'd return with my ticket—which he did, five minutes later.

I then stood on the boat and watched the man walk away with the only possessions I had left, except for a few counterfeit pesos and the sweaty clothes I had on. But it didn't matter; I was another step closer to the island and that made it all worthwhile.

SEVEN

I WASN'T SURE about the legitimacy of my ticket, so I slept on the deck of the boat with several other vagabonds in order to go unnoticed by security officers. I caught a few of the others smiling and staring at me as if to say, *what on earth are you doing way out here*? It would've been hard to explain, so I simply returned their smiles.

I missed the island. I missed my home. I missed Rene and his family. Most of all, I missed the girl. And this time, I knew I wouldn't be facing rejection. I knew she loved me, so this would be a sure thing. I could finally pour my heart out to a woman and not have my soul ripped out in return.

I entered into a deep sleep and dreamed about her. We were playing on the green lawn of the mansion with several small children of mixed ethnicity. They were our children, I supposed. She was so great around kids and it was enjoyable just watching her throw them into the air and catch them, smiling all the while. I was falling more and more in love with her by the minute, if that was possible.

I woke up when someone kicked me. It was bright daylight.

"Kano," said an older man. "We here."

I jumped to my feet and saw that we had, indeed, docked in Surigao. I felt a surge of energy knowing that the Island of Ted was only an hour away. I raced down the ramp, catching a lot of stares on the way, and blasted onto the landing. I had told Nako my approximate date of arrival and was surprisingly on schedule despite the recent hardships. I looked around the docks but didn't see his boat; there were too many around. My pulse surged as I heard the sweetest sound in the world—that of my friend's voice.

"Boss, over here!"

I turned and saw that smiling, Yoda-like, Japanese cargo boat captain.

"Nako!"

I grabbed him in a tight hug, which took him by surprise. I was entirely too sentimental these days.

"I'm glad you back, boss. No one to play baseball with. Rene doesn't have the arm."

I laughed. He began sniffing me.

"It's a long story," I said. "Let's go grab something to eat and find a decent place to pick up an outfit."

"You want to go shopping now?"

I pointed to my clothes and said, "This is all I have left. Besides, I need to find a place to freshen up."

We hit the local mall and I told Nako about the nightmarish trip to get there. I cleaned up in a hotel bathroom and changed into my new outfit, remembering to remove the tags first. I told Nako I'd pay him back once I got a chance to call the bank and straighten them out. Nako and I ducked into a seafood restaurant by the docks to grab some food before heading out to the island. I needed some fuel in my system after a day of famine and I wanted to pull Lanie aside as soon as we got there so I could tell her everything.

Nako scanned his menu and shot a glance up toward me.

"So what bring you back after all this time? I thought you never come back."

"Well," I started. "It took being away to realize where my home really was."

"That's great, boss. So you back for good?"

"Yep," I said with a big grin. "For good."

He nodded, glad to hear it. "So what you miss the most?"

"Of course, Lanie," I said.

Nako's expression changed sharply. He stared into my eyes and then looked down at his hands.

"What? What is it?"

He took a long moment, his eyes avoiding mine.

"Ted, I don't… I don't know how to say this to you. But Lanie is not there."

"Wait… what?" I said, my lips trembling.

"Ted, she leave three months ago."

"She's not on the island? Nako, I came back for her. Where is she? Can we go to her? You have a boat! We can...."

Nako continued looking down solemnly and said, "That's not so possible, boss."

"Why? Where is she?" I said in a panic.

"Rene told me she met a guy in Iloilo. I think they move in together. Ted, I'm very sorry to tell you this. But Lanie is not on the island and... I think she is also pregnant."

The wind was sucked out of the room. I felt a knot in my throat and a sear of heat in my eyes. I took a breath to make sure I was still alive.

I looked down at my menu but couldn't see anything. My vision was blurred.

"Boss, did you come back here for Lanie?"

My head swam and I wanted to puke.

"Yes. I did."

I barely managed to get the words out. Nako then snapped his fingers to get my attention and I finally met his gaze.

"You came all this way for a girl?"

"Yes. I was going to marry her."

Deep sadness penetrated Nako's face. His countenance was grave. It looked like he was feeling my pain. My heart was breaking in half.

"How could she do this?" I thought. I was angry with her. I was angry with Rene for letting her go. But then, slowly, I realized that it was all my fault. I had done this to us. I was the one who left her there with no hope of return. I told her I would write to her and I never did. God knows I picked up a pen and tried several times. But I was afraid of ruining her life and now I had ruined both of our lives. It was intolerable. My entire life flashed before my eyes in the span of a second and I felt my soul crumble. Of all the mistakes I'd made in my life, this is one from which I would not recover.

In utter sincerity, Nako looked at me with pitiful eyes and said, "It's all right, boss. Cause I'm playing joke on you."

"Holy hell!" I shrieked to myself. I wanted to kill him. What a bastard! I threw my spoon at him and saw twisted delight reflecting in his eyes. With friends like this, who needed enemies?

EIGHT

A LIGHT MIST hugged the island as Nako and I docked. He was like a giddy teenager and I, despite the arduous travel and emotional roller coaster, was much the same. Stepping onto the Island of Ted, I felt reborn. It had been a few months since I left and it took me exactly that long to realize where my home truly was.

As Pops used to say, "Home is here, and it goes with you."

For most of my adult life I had fought to understand that veiled statement from Pops, but only at that moment did it become lucid. Home was Lanie, wherever she was. And right now, she was a hundred yards away. It was difficult to contain my excitement as Nako and I entered that familiar forest of palm trees and I smelled the beautiful, fresh night air that only seemed to exist here. As we hit the clearing and I saw the house glowing in the distance, I had to stop and take a deep breath.

Nako, my first *real* friend on the planet, gave me a comforting pat on the back. He seemed to know what I was going through. It was a sobering moment. We then moved forward and approached the house.

Questions flooded my mind at lightning speed. What would I say to her? Would she react warmly? Would she be angry?

I suddenly found myself standing at the front door of the house. Nako saw that I wasn't moving—I was stuck, frozen—so he rang the doorbell for me.

In my mind I laughed, once again, at the irony of a doorbell on the Island of Ted, something that seemed less ironic now.

Rene swung the door open with wide, bewildered eyes and was about to yell when Nako and I both shot a finger to our lips: we wanted this to be a surprise. Rene smiled and led us inside. The house was warm and smelled of delicious food coming from the kitchen. I waved to the children as I walked past them, telling them to be careful not to say anything. Rene then led me to the kitchen.

And then I saw her.

Lanie was removing a roast from the oven when she looked up and saw me standing there. Lynette put her hand to her chest in surprise, and then grabbed the pan from Lanie, who continued to stare at me in a way that was hard to read. I had no idea what to say and the house had become very still and quiet. Every eye in the room was now fixed on the two of us.

"Hi," I said clumsily.

She nodded with a half-smile that told me things had changed between us. She didn't look angry, but she wasn't going to leap into my arms either.

I looked into her eyes and said, "Can we talk in private? Please?"

She stared at me for a moment, then nodded and moved toward the back door. I looked at Rene, who offered me a friendly shrug, before following her outside.

When I stepped onto the bamboo deck and let the door close behind me, I saw Lanie standing near the edge, looking out into the dark forest. I felt as though that special thing that she and I had shared before was not present. Time had not worked in my favor.

Not having the nerve to face her, I spoke to her back. "I'm sorry that I left, Lanie. It wasn't because of you or anything you did. It was my own insecurity."

I saw that her arms were folded but I wished so badly to see her face. I wanted to know if she was angry, or sad, or frustrated.

I took a step closer and said, "I came back... and you're the reason. I'm back because I never want to be away from you ever again, even for a moment."

She stood at the edge of the deck with her back to me, arms folded, refusing to offer me the slightest reaction. I began to feel ashamed. It was the same feeling I'd had the day I expressed my love for Teresa. I only wished that Lanie would say something, even to curse at me or call me an idiot.

"You have every right to be mad at me. The way I left… it wasn't right. It was selfish. And it won't happen again."

The words sounded stupid as I said them. She hadn't given me so much as a hint that she even *wanted* me to stay this time. A long silence fell between us, and I heard only the sound of crickets taunting me.

"Kano?" she said in a voice so soft I could barely hear it.

I took one step closer. "Yes?"

She turned around slowly to face me, her arms still folded. It was hard to see her face in the dark.

"I'm not staying," she said carefully.

My heart raced and I knew in that moment that I had made the mistake of a lifetime by leaving. The words trembled as they left my mouth, "Lanie, can I ask?"

She smiled, briefly, before straightening her expression and nodding "yes."

"Why?" was all I said.

She looked at her feet, the night breeze gently blowing her hair in and out of her eyes, making it hard to look at her.

"Kano, I accept a job. Rene and the others don't have use for me now. Nako take good care of them… bring them what they need."

I was hurt, but how could I ask her to stay now? I had already screwed things up by one act of selfishness and I wasn't ready to do it again.

"What kind of job?" I asked, fighting back waves of emotion. I was happy for her, but the pain in my voice was difficult to hide.

"It's with an organization," she said softly. "There is much travel."

I nodded, "I see. But it will make you happy?"

She nodded "yes" and the wind lifted the hair from her eyes. That's when I saw tears. She smiled but didn't try to hide them.

"When are you leaving?" I asked, the hurt in my voice now even more obvious.

"One week more."

Her voice trembled as she spoke. I wanted so badly to give her a hug and never let her go. She took a step closer to me with eyes glistening.

"I'm happy for you, Lanie. I am."

The tears spilled out onto her cheeks and she wiped her face with her sleeve.

"You saved my life," I said without thinking.

She waved her hand at me dismissively.

"When you came to visit me after Manny died... I don't even know what you said to me, but the sound of your voice... no one has ever spoken to me that way before. It changed me."

Her eyes went down to my chest and then she spoke in a tone I'd heard only once before. "Ted, you save forty lives in your house. You always trying to save people… wherever you are, you always try to save people. I don't know why you don't see this about yourself. But doesn't matter, kano. I see. We are the same. It's why we clicked together." She drew in a breath and continued, "You are the most decent and heroic man I ever knew."

I couldn't believe she was saying such kind things to me after I'd deserted her so many months earlier. She should've been cursing me for what I did.

"And you," I started. "Do you know how I see you?"

She looked at me with shy, wondering eyes.

"I love you."

The moment the words left my mouth, Lanie took a step away from me. I didn't know if she was hurt or just surprised, but the words seemed to jolt her backward. Her face was unreadable and once more I heard only the sound of island crickets.

Then I saw a small grin forming on her lips and she said, "Ah… so what you mean to say is… *mahal kita.*"

My mind immediately flashed back to our first embarrassing encounter in the tent. I extended my hand, just like before.

"Mahal kita. I'm Ted."

Lanie moved closer to me, her body almost touching mine. She wore a mischievous grin. "You know what I'm gonna say now. I love you too, kano."

I lowered myself and she gave me the sweetest hug I've ever felt. I saw Rene and the others watching us from inside the house. I gave him a "thumbs up" signal, and he threw me a wink. The villagers looked so happy for us.

Lanie broke our hug and took a step back.

"Kano, I can't stay on the island. My work... it's not here. I will travel to dark places..."

"I know," I replied.

"So where this leave us?"

Her eyes searched mine, wanting answers. I simply smiled and said, "Home is wherever you are. You are my home."

"Kano," she started, short of breath. "I can't ask that of you. Is too much. I can't ask."

"We'll be in those dark places together. You and me. Wherever life brings us, we'll be side by side."

"You don't know what you're asking."

"Rene is ordained, right?"

She stopped suddenly, and gave me a curious look.

"Why you ask that?"

"We're leaving in a week. Is that enough time to plan a wedding?"

After a few seconds of silence, Lanie smiled and nodded, "We know how to party on Island of Ted."

• • •

Lanie and I said our vows on the wooden dock, with Nako as my best man. Since Lanie's father was no longer alive, Rene decided to give her away. It was an emotional moment and I had to loan Nako a hankie to dry his eyes. For a boat captain who braves the rough seas for a living, he's a bit of a softy. All of the villagers applauded from the beach as I finally brushed the hair from Lanie's face and kissed her peachy lips. It was like celebrating with old friends. Or better yet, with new family.

EPILOGUE

THE PLANE LANDED at Abraham Gonzalez International Airport in Ciudad Juarez at nine o'clock in the morning on a sweltering day. No longer fearing C-grade travel, I hit the ground running with my taxi driver as we embarked on a three-hour drive to an insignificant little nameless town in the Mexican desert.

Pops used to talk of his fondness for these people but until I met Rene and his clan, I never understood that kind of brotherhood. He came here to build a much-needed orphanage and, as he put it in one letter, "Practice true doctrine by taking it out of the lecture halls and into the streets."

When Pops got here, he witnessed a murder on the very first night. Gang violence had been a common occurrence and the police had been bought out years earlier. So it was seriously no-man's land. Thankfully, I didn't know about any of this until after my father had passed or I would've been traumatized by an overactive imagination every time my head hit the pillow.

I had no idea if I was walking into a trap. I hired my interpreter at the airport, so who knows what the guy would do to a hapless American for the right price. I chose to ride in the front seat of the taxi since that allowed me the luxury of jumping out of the car if things got sticky. I had heard of mafia types back in Chicago rigging the back doors of taxis to trap victims for a hit. The paranoia was strong, as was the looming fear in my gut, but I had to see the place where Pops had died. It would hopefully bring some closure and I could finally be at peace about it. Or not.

The taxi pulled over to a sidewalk near a well-groomed garden.

"Strange," I thought. *A garden? Here?*

He looked over to me and said, "It's your stop. I will check into hotel next town over. You have my cell phone when ready."

Wow, I had made it. Alive.

I hopped out of the taxi with nothing but my backpack and cell phone, and strolled the sidewalk into town. A green garden lined the street on both sides, as did well-groomed shrubbery. The place looked nothing like I'd expected. The merchants at their roadside stands all greeted me with warm smiles and waves. *Was I in the Twilight Zone?*

I asked a few of the vendors if they knew anyone who spoke English and they all pointed farther down the road. One of them gave me some roasted plantain and refused to take any money from me. Continuing on, I saw an older Mexican man and woman standing near the shrubs in the town square. Both of them froze when they saw me.

Perhaps these were the English speakers to whom I had been directed.

The elderly man took off his hat as I approached. He looked at me with great curiosity.

"Cómo estás? Habla inglés?"

The old man and woman began talking to one another in Spanish. The man's attention then turned to me and he said, "You remind us of someone."

"My father," I said. "He came here many years ago to build a place for orphans."

At that point the woman raised her shaking hand and pointed to a large, ornate building on top of the hill. I shielded my eyes from the sun and then I saw it. The sign outside the building read, "Casa para Ninos."

Home for children.

I began to beam, a wide smile stretching across my face. The elderly couple understood that I had come here to learn about my father. They took me into their home and, using well-groomed English, were able to articulate all that had happened since my father arrived. They showed me a monument in front of the orphanage, where I saw my dad's face sketched on a marble stone. An inscription read: "Su vida fue intercambiada por los nuestros," which meant "His life was exchanged for ours."

I paid my taxi driver the following day, but didn't require his services. The old man and his nephew, not taking no for an answer, decided to drive me all the way back to the airport so they could share even more stories with me. I had seen the ugliness of life, the tragedy and heartache. But I had also, over the past two years, seen reason for hope.

Lanie stayed in Manila with a friend, since I had insisted on making the trip alone. I kissed her minty lips and touched her nose before promising to return in once piece. Although I'd let go of many fears over this protracted journey, she was still precious cargo. Precious and stubborn. The girl has a way of running headlong into danger, as her job often demanded, but she now had me to block the path of danger—at least when I could.

I had abandoned my career in movies, opting instead for the life of a journalist. Might as well put that degree to use. I was offered a monthly column for Esquire. Occasionally I jotted down some fiction too, and Lanie proved to be a great muse. She had strange dreams all the time, which she insisted on telling me about in great detail. Whenever I was at a sticking point in the story, I'd ask her if she'd had any interesting dreams lately. That always got things flowing again.

I chose the life of a writer because it allowed me and Lanie to travel with her organization. It was always an eye opening experience when we left our luxurious community home on the Island of Ted and hit the most impoverished corners of the country. But it was fulfilling work, with never a dull moment. After traveling together with Lanie for months on end, we'd return to the Island to be with family for a while.

The girls would always make a big feast and we'd sit around, eating and telling stories. In those moments, I often remembered Manny. He was the first one I had met on the Island and it hurt to know that he wasn't there to see me and Lanie exchange vows. It was Manny who had introduced me to the Filipino custom of courting, without which I may have entirely blown my chances with the girl.

I missed that kid a lot. He was someone whose face I longed to see and I had full confidence that we'd be racing again one day. And he'll probably still beat me.

The Island of Ted

Author's Website:
www.jasonthewriter.com

———————————

Other books by Jason Cunningham:

All American Addict

The Lamp Trilogy

PHANTOM FICTION

PUBLISHING

Nashville